850

Versatility is

HIMMELFARB

HIMMELFARB

A Novel

MICHAEL KRÜGER

Translated by Leslie Willson

George Braziller

NEW YORK

First published in the United States of America in 1994
by George Braziller, Inc.

English translation copyright © 1994 by Leslie Willson
Originally published in German

Copyright © 1993 by Residenz Verlag, Salzburg und Wien
under the title *Himmelfarb*

For information, write to the publisher:
George Braziller, Inc.
60 Madison Avenue
New York, NY 10010

Library of Congress Cataloging-in-Publication Data

Krüger, Michael, 1943-
    [Himmelfarb. English]
    Himmelfarb / Michael Krüger ; translated by Leslie Willson.
        p. cm.
    ISBN 0-8076-1363-0
    I. Willson, Leslie. II. Title.
    PT2671.R736H5613 1994
    833'.914—dc20   94-16859
                                                         CIP

Printed in the United States of America

Design by Claire Pinkham

Also by Michael Krüger

The End of the Novel

The Man in the Tower

Diderot's Cat

HIMMELFARB

"The whole being of the old man was actually as though created to arouse my anthropological craving to the extreme."

FG

I

WHEN I SAW his handwriting, I thought immediately of his hands. Clumsy hands for the skinny, haggard-looking body, hands that stuck out of his tight cotton shirt like shovels. The nails were always dirty and lacerated from the tedious operations to remove the sand fleas that had buried themselves with partiality in the cuticles. Then, too, once again I saw again the stiff first joint of the little finger on his right hand, which he had presumably broken in childhood and which had been curiously kinked since then and in shaking hands was irritating when the hand wouldn't quite fit, so that you were always tempted to grip again, whereby a normal, quick, civilized handshake was already botched. There had been people, whom we had run into several times on our trips, who had offered their hand to him with only a single shake, whereas they shook my hand twice as long right in front of him.

And now I see his face before me again, his gray eyes, which were full of sprinkles of yellow, so that, especially if you did not know him, you had to keeping looking into his eyes to try to figure out the reason for the strange effect of his glance. I suddenly remember the relieved expression of an Indian girl whom we had found in the middle of the forest emaciated and naked, with obscured eyelids crawling with ants and flies, which he shooed off with his stiff finger. I see how with infinite slowness, as though in slow motion, she opened her eyes and actually should have fainted at the sight of a white man, but only looked at him mutely, looked into his eyes submissively. An eye healer from Galicia, from whom emanated a downright offensive calmness.

Gaping at the envelope and feeling the handwriting with my fingers, I remember the whole scene. We had brought the girl with great effort to our camp, where she was treated with all the procedures of the medical knowledge at our disposal. I watched my companion make infusions, lay leaves on the sores, wash the girl's body carefully. Two *caboclos* were enjoined not to let the gentle and completely fearless sick girl out of their sight. Very soon he was able to come to an understanding with her. She told him her life story, which he wrote down painstakingly; but when I asked what she had told him, he was evasive. Her statements were meant only for him. The idea that her story belonged to him alone had aroused my envy. No matter how much I had tried to catch something of her story, I had not been successful. Only he understood the people whom we encountered, and even when she spoke with me, he had to interpret her story.

The girl cooked for us and prepared drinks. She ingratiated herself especially with the *caboclos* and the Indians with a pale-yellow, tart beer that she made out of crushed and ground corn, that she covered with hot water and boiled, adding certain leaves and herbs, and then let ferment. If you had not watched its preparation, the brew was refreshing, and if you drank it in modest amounts, it also did not have the devastating effect that it had on many of our guides, who experienced considerable drunkenness with states of delirium and for up to a week afterwards were of no use to us or to anyone else since they showed up groaning and reeling and were racked by diarrhea. She never revealed which herbs she mixed into the corn mash, as in general and quite in contrast to the other Indians who lived with us—pitiable creatures without learning or restraint and of limited intelligence—she made use of astonishing ancient lore that she wanted to share with no one, at any rate not with me.

What is being bestirred again in my mind is strange and alarming: how the writing on an envelope brings light into the darkest corner of memory, how details that have not been touched for fifty years appear inordinately sharp. A tender mating call and everything is ready. Everything is always present—mute, unused, but present—in order to be able to correct life's course at a specifc moment. I felt physically how I began to resist the change. Up until the moment when I received this letter, I had felt myself to be the sure victim of death. I had surrendered—or the man who in me and in my name conducted negotiations with death had admitted his weakness. I did not wish for a rapprochement, rather for a slow ebbing. And now? Now everything was happening effortlessly, now the dark chamber was casting image after image into my uneventful present, dedicated to closure. Probably I had always been waiting to be accosted and recognized. I lived just waiting for that moment, when finally I could remove my mask and say: *So, now I can reveal myself.*

And now I see him, in the bar in São Paolo in which we had met to get acquainted, raise a glass to his mouth, see the stiff little finger protruding into the air. Suddenly I realize that all his gestures, his every incidental movement, are stored in me, and that every attempt in the past to obliterate that record has only sealed the source so that it now can gush forth all the more unrestrained. And while I stare at the envelope that bears my name in his handwriting, I see him sitting in a piragua writing in his journal, see how he fills the account book, wrapped in oilcloth, for page after page with his tiny handwriting, his bird scratchings—black-lined paper, the page numbers at the top over a thick red line, 380 pages. When he had arrived at the last page, he had begun to write in the margins from the back to the front so that the pages, looked at superficially, had the effect of dark surfaces, like the dense hatching of a mentally ill person, and finally also the end pages were filled with his scribbling. A book completely inscribed, which could be decoded lovingly only with the greatest exertion, with a love that resembled penance. You—I—could not read those pages. I had to translate them word for word, transfer them from the ink into a language of experience.

This journal of our two-year journey, which was followed by a second journal, now lies in a safe deposit box in my bank, and as though compelled, I opened the right drawer of my desk and felt among disorganized papers—among which was also my will, which probably would have to be changed again after I read the letter— for an envelope with the key to the bank box, which I also found, to my relief. I took it out and rubbed my thumb over the notched web of the key until it hurt, as though with such a movement I meant to stop my memory, because not for the world did I want during the life I had left to take that oilcloth book into my hand again— not even to destroy it.

The life I had left?

Twenty years after my death, so it said in my will, the journal might be made available for research—for that long it was to be kept locked up in the Museum of Natural History, to which I have bequeathed my library and my collected writings and correspondence in the event of my death. The century should be past and with it the history of journeys on our planet, which from then on could be looked up only in books. For a long time I was indifferent about whether the story of my magnum opus would be discovered after my death, on the one hand because I no longer had my heart in the future of my profession, and on the other hand because I had no descendants who would have to suffer because of the revelation. I still always say obstinately "my field" when I mean ethnology, although it is neither my field nor does it even still exist as a field. There are perhaps a few ethnologists, a few crazy travelers who for good reasons leave their milieu, their insipid prevailing social system to expose themselves to what is foreign, but there has been no ethnology for a long time. The field is wiped out, pulverized in the progress of the sciences. What is foreign has disappeared with the foreign. Probably the postman or the lady gardener across the street, the woman with the small head, is more foreign than any Hopi Indian, who at the end of the month picks up his check so he can get drunk for three days. The sciences, which have blanched us and talked us to death, have left behind an alien, a strange creature that cannot be compared through any analogy with a human being. The common sun has set, and in the shadowless plain a few shapes scurry about that can easily be observed. Down with ethnology, down with journeys!

I had already put one part of my correspondence in order, when severe heart aberrations had appeared, shortly after my seventieth birthday, and I had to assume I would not live very long. I had filled and labeled sixty-four green cartons, which stood in two wobbly piles in my study. Even my correspondence with Annibal Valcerama about intoxicants (especially *niopo*)—which I had recently had in my hands again in order to write a letter to the editor against an especially arrogant article in our ethnological association newsletter—fills its own carton and is, in its substance, thoroughly suited to justify a special publication. The whole correspondence on intoxicants, especially my observations about the effect of hallucinogenic mushrooms, is spread over several depositories and can be decoded through a complicated system of references that I had included in photocopy in each carton. Since I refused to acquire a computer, my entire writings were done by hand on cards—a contrived system, the appropriate attention to which would provide bread and butter for many students.

When, for my seventy-fifth birthday, I was offered the honor of several so-called ethnological professorial chairs (two of which I could not or did not want to refuse, for reasons incomprehensible to me today), I had to interrupt the five-year task of cataloging, because of the ceremonial lectures I had to write, in order to submerge myself again in the old papers that in part had been stored for thirty years, held together by brittle twine, untouched under a furry layer of dust. The more the world was lost with finality, the more persistently were the universities interested in my trips during the forties. And the more bleak and repugnant the present state of society appeared, the more were people desirous of cramming one doctoral hat after another onto my head for my depictions of the bleak and repugnant condition of the Brazilian Indians. Moreover, I had the impression of being draped with that academic frippery only because, uninvolved with the ridiculous methodological disputes that despoiled the field and brought forth no new knowledge about the early history of man, I usually acknowledged the receipt of another hat with a new story that in each instance, according to the status of the professorial chair, I more or less colorfully illuminated. With broad and complacent verbosity, saturated with so-called observations, I invented a history for the Indians that admittedly bristled with notorious unreliability and confusion, a dissolute orgy of the most colossal dilettantism that was nevertheless suited to furnish the totally vacuous, decontaminated listeners—who customarily turned up at such semi-academic celebrations—with a feeling of having been there. The result was correspondence that could no longer be stayed.

My syntheses were always more or less pretentious, mostly presumptuous and untenable, and my vanity in showing off my erudition at appropriate and inappropriate passages destroyed my address even when I really did have something to communicate. I liked best to speak about religion, the spiritual lore of the Indians, because with this theme I could appeal to the bad consciences of my audience. But the less substance I brought forward, all the more eagerly did people follow me. I intend to investigate this phenomenon separately, although there can be no doubt about the comment of an English friend, which he shared with me in the last letter before his death: "Today, in the middle of the twentieth century, the living tradition of spiritual lore is as good as erased. The organized centers of spiritual collection have been shattered everywhere. 'Progress and civilization,' it seems, are gaining acceptance along the whole line, and a new race of men, to whom all this is of no consequence, populates the earth."

At the old English universities you had to deal with cannibals warily. In small towns in southern Germany, where ethnology is taught as a kind of higher tourism, I might have seen in my untenable fantasies a human leg hung from a calabash under the horrified eyes of a Spanish missionary, under the covetous eyes of the Indians.

On my eightieth birthday I had declined all honors with a reference to my health, although, according to my own assessment, I am today in far better shape than in the previous ten years. Above all, the onerous, anxiety-producing heart troubles had faded away. Now, except for a vast quantity of birthday missives that were divided up into three small piles—those to answer, those to answer sooner or later, those not to answer under any circumstance—I had no pressing work to finish and had looked forward to the further cataloguing of my writings, when three days after my birthday the postman, a very pleasant man to whom I gave money or autographed editions of my works for occasional extra chores, brought me a letter that, to put it mildly, brutally stopped me from any work and put me into a state of agitation the likes of which I have not known for many years.

It was a letter from the man with whom, about fifty years ago when war was raging in Europe, I had traveled through the Brazilian jungle, in the damp gloom of which I had last seen him in 1941. To be precise, in the rundown cottage of a former Capuchin priest who, for all kinds of good reasons (which he tried to explain to us in endless harangues), did not want to return to his faith because it had no answers to the senseless metaphysical questions with which he wrestled. But to make up for that, he had the natives—raw, mischievous individuals for whom he held mass three times a week—slave for him for the greater glory of a God completely incomprehensible and indifferent to them. A bad accident on the part of my traveling companion had forced us to spend more than three months in the mission, which served willy-nilly also as our station. And to escape the gruesome theological kitsch of the priest, my companion had asked my permission to dictate his travelogue to me, based on the expansive notes in his oilcloth booklet.

We worked feverishly, if you will permit the expression. Two delegations, which we had sent out to the nearest city for help, had not returned. Probably they had drunk themselves into insensibility in the first bar. When it finally looked as though my companion would not recover from the bad infection and other infirmities that accompanied it, I packed the oilcloth booklet and the manuscript in my handwriting, that had come into being based on it into a watertight bag, and with two *caboclos* and an Indian set off, not without leaving behind the promise to publish the manuscript after the war as a book in his name, should the author die. He wanted to preserve his name; that's about how his whispered testament sounded. I had enjoined the disreputable priest to send me news about the state of recovery of my traveling companion by way of the German consulate in São Paolo, and specifically to the University of Leipzig, where after my return I wanted to finish my studies. Still, I neither received any news, nor did I really get a degree. Inquiries about the priest revealed that he had died, it was said, in 1949.

A few months ago I received in a letter from a Czech whom I had once met in Brazil the information that the confused ideas of the priest about the imminent end of the world had in the sixties further made an impression on the theological faculty in São Paolo. But no one had seen the Capuchin again. No one had ever heard anything more of Leo Himmelfarb from Galicia, the eye healer with the immense hands. He lived, hidden under the rubbish of years, only in a dusty corner of my mind, in many a moment suddenly illuminated by a spark of my memory: Then a man beckons to me from a seemingly infinite distance, an apparition, and forces me to open up my eyes so that this shape—physically becoming more and more clarified—can dissolve into reality.

After the war I went to Munich and worked in an insurance company office, where I soon became sales manager. Everybody wanted to get insured after the war, as though in that way they could escape the final destruction that threatened. I earned a lot of money. After 1953 at yearly intervals I published several novels and travelogues about my excursions into the Brazilian jungle, which even today are reprinted again and again and translated into all civilized languages. From the fees that then, after leaving the agency, I received as a freelance writer, as a travel book author, I bought the house in which I still live today. In my long, successful career—if I may so characterize my own work of repeating the same thing over and over—I made only one mistake that could now be my undoing: I dedicated the first of my books, of which nothing but the title originated with me, to the memory of my friend Leo Himmelfarb. After fourteen licensed editions around the world, it has now been translated into Hebrew. And his letter came from Haifa.

I see him before me, how he crosses the campsite with his quick, short steps, which in the course of his illness became more and more plodding, more and more shuffling and solitary, his flecked eyes catching everything uneasily; how he now gives good advice and now has something explained to him, maybe an improvement of the water conduits he had built with the Indians and that he supervised proudly, although the result was more than unsatisfactory; how with a corn leaf-wrapped cigarette in his mouth, his hands in his trouser pockets, with an ironic smile he observes the plantings, which must be maintained against the might of the primeval forest. I see a melancholic gambler with serious intentions, the straw hat sitting on the back of his head, leaving his forehead free for attacking insects that he slaps away nonchalantly with his fingers. I see him in inordinate clarity. I don't see myself.

"It was your wish to penetrate into this wretched Paradise," he said to me when I wanted to give up. "You wanted to hunt up these forgotten human beings, not I. You wanted to unscramble the chaos of their myths, with arrogance and frivolity. I wanted to become a writer, that was all. My succumbing kingdom is called Galicia. I was interested in its people and wanted to record their stories. The story of the scissors grinder and his religious mania. The stories of the rabbis and their interpretation of the Scripture. But people like you prevented me from doing that. The difference is that I'm free. I could abandon you tomorrow. But you? For you it will be hard to retrace the path you have taken—you are chained to a mission. I will find a room in one or another of these damp cities. I will buy a carton of cigarettes, wine, and paper with your German money and will write a German novel that will be read after the war ends, a novel about you, the eth-nologist in the hammock, who is repulsed by the unclean-liness of the Indians and by the insects that suck these poor, cast-aside creatures dry."

And then he laughed the bitter laugh of the outlaw, of one spat out by history, pushed his hat back farther on his head, and bent over a task again, whereas I lay in my hammock, speechless with anger and shame. After all, he was my employee. After all, I, the fellowship holder of the Third Reich, had given work to him, the destitute

Jew. But every time I was about to say something in my own defense, he cut me short.

"It's too hot for a real defense," he said then. "Under these conditions it's better to hate in silence. Then it will pass by quicker, too."

II

I CAN'T RELY on my memory anymore. For some time now there suddenly appear in my imagination images of cities, bodies, and things that I believe I know very well but without knowing to which concrete situation in my life I should attribute them. I walk along streets that do not belong to the city I would like to remember, see the village from which I come enclosed by a massive cordillera dipped into scarlet-red light, speak a language I don't know to people whose names I have forgotten. Dismaying projections of an imagination enfeebled by age, incoherent interlinkages, restrained by no chronology. Words from indigenous languages, faces that, hardly identified, slip away again, become wraiths. A merging of magnitude and limit. For a few seconds my memory loses all restraint. It produces events that I see before me with super-clarity without being able to detect myself in those scenes. I no longer occur, am extinguished in a life that I, one might believe, did myself lead. A whimsical management of mind, incomprehensible work in the darkness of a cybernetic program that appears to manage without me. Sometimes I have to laugh, when my fantasy's throw of the dice casts me into situations that I can in no way have survived. Sometimes I fall into enraptured astonishment because in strange surroundings I recognize details that themselves had ponderous consequences for future experiences. But mostly it is embarrassing for me to stumble around in that unknown landscape of my existence. It is as though before my final exit I had to display everything that I have seen, thought, and felt, but had no more time to present the swarm in an orderly fashion. A true absurdity.

Today a face pursues me that stands before me in all its detail with no body far or near. A phantom face. It sits opposite me, for example, in a rattling train, somewhere in the mountains, and when I ask what its name is, repeat the question more urgently again and again, it laughs and lunges away, vanishes. Vanishes so completely in one of the brackish pools of my memory that I cannot remember even details of its physiognomy. And while I try grimly and somewhat ridiculously to imagine the jolting train that was still propelled by wood, my gaze on the meagerness of the landscape, while suddenly I can see clearly as, bent forward, my hands outstretched, I start to call out something to a person, abruptly that very face appears at a festival in the jungle. Everyone is drunk, even the women. There are coarse, abominable scenes, which are interceded by the unknown face. I have no idea where I ever met it. So as not to become completely mad, I decide to give the face as a specimen to a doctor, whom I can no longer physically bring to mind, whose history and circumstances of life however are clearly before my eyes. He was living together with a group of Indians— Cayuas or Cayapós, if I'm not mistaken—about fifteen kilometers west of us. The Indians, it occurs to me now, were wearing shirts and pants with a European cut; the women, sack-like long dresses. Sometimes, more out of curiosity, they came to us for mass, but generally held on to their old notions.

When Leo and I once, because of stormy weather,

had to stay overnight with them in an indescribably stinking hut, an especially business-minded Indian offered us his daughters for the night, charming creatures who under their ready-raised sack dresses wore a bark triangle on a hip cord and a kind of woven mesh over their breasts. We politely declined. Thereupon, little by little, a dozen more girls were offered, the youngest of them no older than twelve or thirteen years at the most. It became more and more difficult to find reasons for our refusal.

And while I see quite clearly how Leo with raised hands rejects the girls with a smile, I suddenly also see before me the laughing face of the doctor, to whom our steadfastness obviously seems comical: his cheerless, drunken eyes, his yellow skin, and his thin, insect-bitten throat on a curiously boyish body. And at the same time I realize that I must look for a different body for my phantom face. Maybe I'm ill, senile. In any event, I can no longer reconstruct my life exactly—everything crumbles away.

There are said to be people who into an advanced old age, until the end, can account for the reasons for their actions, who are always composed and garner recognition for their self-composure, but I do not belong to them, I never belonged to them. Perhaps out of inertia, out of ennui. I was dominated by the coincidences that I could not accommodate in my ideas about life. I used to hide my shame about my lack of proficiency under a shell of arrogance; now I surrender to it without hesitation. And since my memory has abandoned me and confuses me with unexpected stimulations, I see only fissures, repudiations, rubble. Everything is then cleared out, bare.

Sometimes I feel such a great revulsion rising in me that I can breathe only with difficulty. But I have no idea from what depths this melancholia comes. You see, I don't believe that my fragmentary memories really weigh heavily on me. They are putting me to the test, want to challenge me, but when I succeed in repressing them, then they're not dangerous to me either. The revulsion must have another source. But however much I try to find it, it remains hidden. Am I afraid of no longer existing?

The face. The hut of the doctor. The whitish maggots that we had to eat up alive. The crooked crucifix on the filthy wall covered with countless insects. The snorting pigs chewing at our packs. The dirty, disconcerted girls. Leo's ironic face. The merciless swarms of mosquitoes. The big-hearted Indian (I can't stand big-hearted people). The hate, the gray, crippling stupidity. The situation divested of any charm. Perhaps all of that, taken together, produces the choking revulsion. Perhaps it took more than forty years for the poison out of all these details to collect in order to demoralize me in the end.

As long as I lived from my memories, as long as I could write them down again and again, change them, improve them, I had no distress in my life. But now that everything has turned into flow, movement, trembling dissolution, now that the chaotic, now-unanchored memories plague me and undercut any order and hierarchy, I'm developing into a frightened child. Fright is returning. It covers me like a thick carpet. There are no more words to write it away. No word to keep it at bay.

But now that this letter is lying before me, I am forced to pull myself together once more. For the last time. Afterward, let fright close my eyes.

33

III

I WAS THE FIRST to arrive at the unfriendly joint that had been mentioned to me as the meeting place. Not far away from my hotel, it lay in an area of São Paolo in which many Europeans resided, mostly Italians and Englishmen, but apparently also Germans, as I could hear right after my entrance. "You won't do that. You won't go that far," I heard a man call out as I appeared through the beaded curtain that separated the street drenched with harsh sunlight from the dark, smoky room in which a handful of people were sitting at a few tables, more men than women. Sudden quiet. Unusually ponderous, as though I had been set down there, I stood in the door, my right hand clasping the greasy beads, smoothing my hair self-consciously with my left. Here a secret tribunal was meeting, before which I had to make a good impression. In the air hung a heavy odor of stale alcohol that deepened the depressed mood even more. I had already become accustomed to the fact that in this wild city a human being was not necessarily considered something that could adorn the world, but in the schnapps bars even the last remainder of cordiality seemed no more in demand. Something obstinate and mistrustful emanated from the people, who soon again softly continued their impetuous conversations accompanied by quick gestures, after they had obviously decided to consider me a harmless customer.

As though over boggy ground I walked to and sat down at the only free table, a rectangular wooden table that you would not touch if you did not want to stick fast like the flies that were tumbling around like drunkards. Everything about me was wrong: my haircut, my face as though frozen, my white suit, even the blue cuffs that peeked out of the sleeves. I'll be carried right out, I thought, like a superfluous decoration. I asked the bartender, who with a wry grimace wordlessly invited me to order, whether Luisa had been there, which seemed to provoke no further reaction from him. He turned away, leaving me alone, but I got nothing to drink. Not for the first time in this country did I have the sheer physically painful feeling of being merely tolerated. My feet were smarting. Here undependability is the most widely distributed virtue, unpunctuality its clearest expression. Everyone promises you the moon and the stars, but if you show signs of accepting the promises, you are maliciously let down. Everyone lies and curses like thunder. Talking big is part of the trappings. So I was suddenly no longer sure whether I was really scheduled to meet with Luisa at just this hour in this odd bar; even she, as a part of this society, preferred such a stormy rhetoric that the essence of her statement, in this case our meeting, was soon muffled.

Luisa was half German. Her mother had been a friend of my Leipzig professor, "almost engaged" (said Luisa), before through marriage she had wound up in this city, at the German school in which her two daughters, Luisa and Vera, had learned German. The family lived in a better section of the city, but Luisa knew her way around the bars downtown that the artists frequented; as she put it, the whole bunch hopeless ne'er-dowells who didn't look like they had ever painted a picture or published a book. Loquaciousness was the iron law of their exchanges. I had often observed that even when nothing more was to be said, when they were empty, they slowly pumped themselves up again so that they finally could find words an incentive for the continuation of the prattle. They stole everything from Europe and disfigured it beyond recognition. Talented thieves, convinced braggarts. They were invulnerable to the temptation of developing an understanding from a rational perspective. But to make up for that they were brilliant and lively, capable of quick indignation and slow forgetting, a self-appointed elite without any mandate who met together every day to eviscerate the newest booty. Luisa was their most prominent challenge.

She talked to them about a "project" that claimed her entire attention and that she could talk about for hours, even if her listeners, as I had learned several times, actually wanted to hold forth on other subjects. Luisa ordained, the others kept their mouths shut, because as a rule she also paid the bill. Her project was the animal soul. Every howler monkey and every kinkajou, every tarantula and every pig had a soul in whose classification, description, and mythical enhancement she invested her entire energy, even if the purpose that seemed to lend wings to her investigation was not completely clear. She wanted to "grasp" what was holy in every animal. But what would happen if she had actually grasped it? I must admit that I was in no way interested in the soul of the curassow, and not only because I didn't even know what it looked like, the bird whose filigreed soul she described with unheard-of rhetorical verbosity; and the small spark that was said to flicker in the bird I did not know swelled to a delirium of incantations. Still, I too always listened with hypocritical attention because Luisa was the only woman whom I knew in this city.

My professor had enjoined me not to seek contact in any way with emigrants, nor with Communists or Jews, or either of them, since the danger existed that they could influence the research that I always had to conduct with the greatest objectivity in order one day to be permitted to wear a German doctoral hat. In his view emigrants were not displaced persons or expellees, rather exclusively preachers, fanatics, or anarchists and could therefore not be objective. The Arms on the Cross are spread above all races and cultures, with the exceptions of Jews and agnostics—his words—whereby I was never certain how serious he was. The professor, who had been a Party member for a few years, strode into the lecture hall with his boots on and greeted us with an outstretched arm, which, even to me, a child of so-called petit bourgeois circumstances, had seemed exaggerated. At the same time, any exaggeration was abhorrent to him, and nothing could upset him more than surprises. His essays after 1936, in contradiction to his previously published writings, were unprecedentedly mediocre and mucked up with hopeless ideologies and, moreover, stood his own research on its head. But since he himself knew this best, he aspired to the objective education of his pupils. Right after the end of the war he hanged himself in the Institute. One of his last, no-longer-published writings, which was posthumously found in his papers, ended with these sentences:

> *Two spirits wrestle for the soul of the German Volk—the spirit of Christ and the spirit of the Jew. If we look at our people as they are today and as they have become, particularly in the last decades, then we must admit with a shudder that the Jewish spirit has already conquered broad domains of the German soul. We have today hardly any reason for arrogance toward the Jews and hardly any right, since so many Germans have fallen*

completely to the Jewish spirit. But we should let their fate be a lesson to us and in it recognize where our path leads if we continue to chase after our seducers instead of pondering about ourselves and the destiny revealed to us by God. Above all, today the preservation of the Christian spirit is entrusted to the German. It is the eternal task of the German. If we thrust Christ from us, as the Jews thrust Him away from themselves because He wanted to be their King, then we shall share the fate of the Jews. Then the living source of our existence will also run dry, and our nationhood will wither from within.

The Aryan creed should help us to understand our own being and to lay aside what is alien. If we make the Aryan creed our own, then we will renounce the Eternal Jew and profess the eternal German.

I was never certain what this earnest, profound, mythically inclined intellectual really thought, he who on the one hand ridiculed the spiritual dry rot of his age, then on the other hand conjured up masculine procedure—pure clarification and an unshakable hierarchy of things, he who charged our Leipzig University with the loss of instinct, program, character, and tradition and at the same time praised its lofty precept of consistency.

Probably his train of thought had jumped the rails. For whenever I recall with what love this man spoke about the Indians of Tierra del Fuego, who were the object of his research, then I have to believe that he had a deeply split personality. A weakling who put on his uniform so that he wouldn't dissolve.

He and his kind are to blame that our branch of study never really got onto its feet again after the war. Englishmen, Frenchmen, Americans wherever you looked. They wanted to compensate on the one hand for the colonial past of their countries and on the other for the fear-inspiring advances of the Western industrial countries, whereby our discipline became the ridiculously fashionable field for culturally weary children of rich parents who scared their families at home with the threat that all the colored peoples of this world would one day take bloody revenge for the Western inability to feed them properly.

Our discipline of study was, in truth, free of any misgivings. It was simply stricken with a bad conscience and, run down like all the humanities or arts, decayed at the roots. Where earlier the plant existed, a multiplicity of forms, there existed now only the dried-out, nodular thickets of theory. No more observation, no patience in perception, no composure in discernment and in description. Only the violence of theory, its cudgeling survey of boundaries that could be crossed only under threat of death. Anyone who has to be an eyewitness to how greatly these disciplines distance themselves from any doubt about their convictions, consolidated through gruesome historical experiences, must get sick to his stomach. They know everything, and everything is false. Anyone who, as I, must enter today's institutions to receive honors is met with an odor of putrefaction from the new architecture. The putrefaction of the present. Even after one year the buildings look like ancient finds, as though from a time when there were still no human beings. One of the chief reasons for the putrefaction was the hope of my Leipzig professor—wearing his boots, with his Party emblem and his Hitler salute—that the world could still be saved through objective science, through patient research. Now it is in the process of suffocating from its so-called knowledge.

I had taken a seat from where I could keep my eye on the entrance. Like sitting in a dark, smoke-filled movie house, I could watch the people who scurried back and forth in front of the entrance, could observe the woolly, waved, slicked-back, and unkempt hair, the Negroes, Indians, Chinese, half-breeds, and whites, and besides could follow the conversation at the next table, which had to do with the question of whether the Party had a chance to intervene in the German altercations. How naïve was the talk with a nasal Rhenish intonation in this dark hole. How gladly I would have joined in as the newcomer just arrived, the man with the latest news, to tell them something about German youth. About myself, for example. But, of course, I said nothing, just listened with inclined head, transfixed, peered anxiously toward the bright rectangle of the door, whisked the flies from the backs of my hands, and waited. It occurred to no one to talk to me. Not even the dirty child of the bartender, who watched me motionlessly from his safe position behind the bar, made a move to come to me after his father shooed him away with a wave of his hand. He took a few awkward steps in front of the bar and stared in my direction like a small, mean, toothless old man.

I wanted out of there, back to Germany. I did not want to sink in the ocean of the unknown that surrounded and troubled me. I was not interested in Indians, those degenerate humans, and their propensity for alcoholism and quarreling. I wanted neither to save them nor damn them; I wanted to describe neither their good points nor their bad ones, which developed so quickly at the first opportunity. I didn't even want to see them.

And then finally Luisa came and immediately changed the situation. She said hello to almost everyone in this catacomb, stroked the head of the suddenly laughing child, here with her bright voice let fall a remark about radical mysticism, there interrupted a somber little transaction, beckoned to the grimy bartender, and finally made her way to my table, greeted me solemnly, and introduced the thin man who had followed her like a shadow: Leo Himmelfarb.

I remember well that I almost could not stand up from shock. Himmelfarb. The idea that I should traverse the primal jungle with a Leo Himmelfarb paralyzed me, and the thought of having to mention in my reports to the Institute that a Leo Himmelfarb had helped me to record genealogical tables made me shudder. I was about to investigate our civilization's state of social infancy for the Leipzig Ethnological Institute, and from among all the people on the earth was taking a Galician Jew as my traveling companion, a writer, as it soon turned out, whose novel, already accepted by a Berlin publisher, could no longer appear in Germany and now would probably never appear. Leo Himmelfarb. A wiry man in a faded suit, a storyteller whose first joint of the little finger of his right hand stood out stiffly because that hand had gotten caught in a hawser cable on a Danube steamer and been crushed. This man, in Luisa's opinion, could now at the expense of the German Reich, which had just expelled him, live on vacation for two years as my assistant.

We ordered a foul-smelling schnapps and scrutinized one another—that is, I scrutinized him. There are decisions in life at which one hesitates a long time because one knows instinctively that life will change because of them, mostly for the worse, and still one makes them. It was impossible for me to have even an intimation of the unpleasant situation into which this man would force me. Yet we by no means limited ourselves to an exchange of civilities. On the contrary. He railed about Germany, scoffed at our government—*your* government, he always said, as though I had formed a government—the German universities, writers, newspapers, in short everything that was German, and he uttered his imprecations with a volume that drowned out all other sounds and increased with every schnapps.

Soon the whole joint was listening to Himmelfarb's tirades and my polite whispering, which sprang out of sheer anxiety that the customers listening in the joint could declare me an enemy and rough me up. After all, I was the enemy to them. At any rate, from my entrance into the bar on, even on the threshold, I had felt different, but interpreted that for my part as superiority, which for the length of my stay was of no advantage but probably fortified me; in those kinds of places each and every thing is constrained to the prevailing level. I had felt foreign but invulnerable, then superfluous, finally as the enemy. The next step was humiliation.

Leo subjected me to a questionable exercise, as though he had as many sources of funds and employment as he wished to pick from, which in no way corresponded to the truth. He was broke. Still, with the most familiar candor he coaxed out of me my political views and domestic circumstances, and in this methodical questioning proceeded so cleverly that I was afraid suddenly that I had concealed something, whereby I kept producing footnotes and addenda to what I had already said and on the whole gave an impression of being hardly equipped for the coming adventure. And when I was finally out of words, when I had nothing more to say and could only shrug my shoulders helplessly as a sign of capitulation, under Luisa's arbitrating eyes Leo set about telling me his life story, which was a horrible story of suffering. He spoke with the clarity that utter exhaustion sometimes produces. Then he stopped abruptly and said, "You are the last person from whom I shall seek understanding. We have a working relationship, if I accept your offer." He said that exactly as though I had already hired him, as though it were a fact that only we two could subjugate the primeval jungle.

And then he lapsed again into his modulation of abuse and talked about the ministry of Christ and its curious apostles who had brought the Cross on gunboats to Brazil, jeered at the powerful, base body of Christian culture that had breathed out its soul, and finished with a vulgar tirade against colonial imperialism, which was nothing more than mean colonial gangsterism. Our errors, mistakes, and vices, the degrading follies of our civilization, which had sunken into materialism, our shameful predatory disposition, finally our ridiculous prejudices about the inferiority of the nonwhite races— "All these sins scream for vengeance!" shouted this skinny man, quickened by alcohol, with violent passion into the smoky, listening room.

47

And after that eruption of the lava of scorn—which included me, of course—he looked at me openly with his curiously beaming, peaceful eyes.

Luisa, too, seemed satisfied.

We ordered another schnapps, clinked glasses, and agreed to meet the next day. I remember dimly that I had remained sitting for a long time in the dusky room, alone as never before in my life but no longer an outcast, with a bottle of schnapps before me that emptied slowly with the setting sun, until my head fell onto the sticky tabletop. Two countrymen from the bar dragged me past the completely indifferent bartender and the unmoving, staring child out into the street and to my hotel, where the next morning, after a night convulsed with chills and nightmares, Leo Himmelfarb, my future traveling companion, woke me for our first organizational meeting.

IV

FOR YEARS I suffered under the depressing delusion of having sired a child with Luisa, and even today, when I believe I have freed myself finally from that childish complex, which for far too long wracked me with devastating feelings of guilt, I occasionally am afraid of being called father by an utterly strange man whom I notice, for example, in the subway because he stares at me intensely. I don't want to discuss my dreams in which I appear as father and disgrace myself. It's always boys who sneak into my fantasies and reveal themselves in difficult scenes as my flesh and blood. Meanwhile, he would have to be a fifty-year-old man, so in any event a conversational partner, but in my dreams he is frozen as an adolescent, as a wild child who wants to bring disorder into my life. I never married. Not from a lack of opportunity; on the contrary, there were phases in my life in which I was able to elude marriage only with difficulty. There is a place in me that no one may enter.

Especially during my early days in Munich, when success pursued me and led me to be incautious, I had several lovers simultaneously. Among themselves and behind my back they had kept in contact, which amounted to absolute surveillance. I was able to escape a lady psychoanalyst who had a long, pale face, whom I still meet occasionally on strolls—she is now over seventy and heavily marked by alcohol—only by giving her lectures in bitter earnest about the advantages of patriarchy, which in the course of time put her into such a rage that hitting it off normally was inconceivable. But it was exactly those stupid speeches about the deficient female, which I loaded up with impudent borrowings from ethnology, that provoked a painter who was friends with the analyst to approach me, which, in ignorance about the friendly connections between the two women, I readily allowed. I became perceptibly depraved as long as women were nearby.

As though under duress I invented the most audacious stories from the history of primitive peoples, and the painter, especially, was determined to hear every far-fetched thing. Early Man was the area that I especially preferred. When Early Man began to bring order into the world through systems of manifestos, woman—the mutilated man—was forced into the second ranks in order to put a stop to sexual anarchy. Such speeches, for which I afterwards cursed myself, had once led the painter to want to submit to me unconditionally, an embarrassing predicament in this very study where I sit even today at my writing desk. She was not a resourceful painter. A watercolor by her hangs in the entryway: *Shadows in the Park,* in which a small, round moon throws a shadow, a dark shimmering shadow, the paradox of which I don't understand even today. With this painter my propensity to get closer to women trickled away, even when with increasing age I occasionally sense the longing and desire to know one of them is at least nearby. Distantly nearby.

Just once I had been invited to Luisa's parents' house, a weary, neglected building in a genteel part of the city, with dirty walls and worm-holed, dusty balconies on which old ladies timorously drank chocolate. The exterior was without the Baroque decoration of the surrounding houses and the interior without comfort or even cleanliness. The house enclosed a shadowy inner courtyard in which flowers, bushes, and vines grew indiscriminately in earthen containers and wooden tubs in such multitudes that, upon my entrance, at first I did not see the people at all who—in my honor—had gathered there. They gave the impression of fruit in an artificial jungle—squash, cucumbers. Even though they hardly spoke my language, most of them considered themselves German, being descendants of the colonists of 1850 in the Blumenau settlement, and one and all were more or less open to the view that the events taking place in Germany were right and proper and stood in harmony with the Christian destiny of the Reich.

The old women, particularly, were conceited and pretentious, even when one sensed the secretly rankling feeling that their claim to superiority over all other peoples, especially the Brazilian hordes, rested basically on a fragile foundation. Behind passions and emotions was concealed the fear of no longer belonging. All the more did these slothful lemurs cling to me, the German from the Reich, and from them I experienced a friendliness that at home I had not observed for a long time in associating with people. They nuzzled me into the iciest stiffness. Luisa's father, a tyrannical misanthrope, said in his short, unsentimental after-dinner speech that if in the future it were to be valid that the world was made by mankind for mankind, then one would have to distinguish between the lazybones who did nothing and the Germans who did something, even if some of the latter had spent time writing nonsensical things that came dangerously close to doing nothing. He meant the Indian research—me.

In fact, in the circle of his friends I had found acceptance and work, but the idea of ending my life as a part of this fragile tableau, even of becoming a gourd in this tropical hothouse, made me exalt the scientific significance of the work that I wanted to bring to a satisfactory conclusion in the name of the Reich. I had never before in my life been in such disagreement with myself, with my suit, my gestures, my short speech of thanks. While speaking I had the feeling of sinking through my shoes because what was false was becoming ever heavier, and when I could finally sit down again, I felt with my hand to see whether the soles were still in one piece. Then we ate: cold fowl, crabs, hard-boiled eggs, and all sorts of remarkable things with a lot of Spanish pepper. Finally a hazardous, warm dish in which half the meat and vegetable market was represented, and behind a massive bush in bloom, fish was being grilled, from which the steam of frying oil spread a suffocating stench.

In addition, they were drinking like fools. On the one hand suspicious-looking liquids in all colors, on the other hand wine, but also grape and sugar schnapps, which caused a furious heat to well up in me, but in the others led to a lulling indolence to which they surrendered only too willingly. This inchoate activity perplexed me at first and led me to exercise restraint, but then all the bodies sprawling lasciviously in the easy chairs provoked me, and I began, to my own astonishment, to challenge with open signs of hate the distrustfully dejected and profoundly silent company. How the person who hissed out of me had crept in without my having noticed was a puzzle to me. The result of my tirade, bullied out of me by melancholy and homesickness, consisted at any rate of the fact that Luisa, who was afraid of a commotion, tore me away from these futile efforts to lead an unexpected conversation by offering to show me the house and had already with both hands dragged a reluctant me out of the threadbare armchair, hooked her arm in mine, and pulled me into a dark hallway and from there out over a gently curving staircase into the garden and onto the street.

We walked a few hours through the humid, heavy evening. My shirt stuck to my body. I carried my jacket over my arm like a waiter after work. I felt unwell in my skin, which for its part stuck to my shirt, in this spooky, evening city, in this oversize country that had nothing to say to me, to which I could say nothing, even if it had listened, and the prospect of having to travel in a few days into the jungle made me so unhappy that for a long time I couldn't get a word past my lips. Luisa commented on the dully brooding houses that stood on the badly paved street: almost exclusively, Germans lived here. The gate to the insane asylum was standing open, so we slipped past two damaged statues that represented Hippocrates and Galen and at once stepped into a colonnade that, resembling the cloisters of a monastery, enclosed a rectangular garden. Bird cries, which at first I took for the meowing of a cat.

Behind an iron grille, standing and lying in a high, badly illuminated room, were the afflicted—mysterious, solitary people, a brooding company from which now and again sharp, aberrant, intimidated cries rose up and slowly ebbed away. White, red, black, and yellow were all mixed together here componentially, about a hundred men, of whom in the prevailing obscurity not one looked as though he would ever be released healed. Taken all in all, this lightly quickened mass did not harmonize with the mental image that a European usually has of inmates of a clinic for nervous disorders. The sight of these men, who gave the impression of being forgotten, gripped me so strongly that I dared breathe only shallowly, sound-lessly, and only when with obscene movements a wild fellow invited Luisa to step closer to the grille was the spell broken. A frightful noise set in, an insanely trium-phant, torrential roar, like the sudden outburst of a thun-derstorm, and even those who had just been squatting lethargically on the ground crept panting, as far as their grimy clothing permitted, to the grille to add their contri-bution to the general uproar with insane sounds and snarling screams. It was like a picture of whose existence one had always known but forbade oneself to look at for good reasons. A burning, breathtaking panic gripped me. I did not want to see the picture. I did not want to die.

We fled, ran through the corridor past the two chipped guardian saints of the physicians' art into the open, without having been noticed by any custodian. Perhaps there were no attendants here. Only at noon and evening a guard who tossed straw through the grille.

Not far away from the insane asylum on a dismal square cock fighters had gathered, scruffy figures made visible like wraiths by a few petroleum lamps. To conclude their shady bets, with their hands they incessantly made strange signs that resembled the language of the deaf and dumb. At the ring sat a fat Indian dripping with sweat, who served as the referee. Then from the dark mass of the spectators two men stepped out who were at first carrying their roosters under their arms like briefcases but then grabbed them by the body with both hands to hold them out toward the other fellow fighter. With cocked, twitching heads the two birds eyed one another until one of them suddenly stretched its head and hacked the other on the comb with a telling blow.

When the neck feathers of both finally ruffled, they were set down on the earth of the dusty arena and expertly appraised, because now the fat Indian began to collect the bets. Luisa played *à la baise* and bet on the smaller, tousled rooster, which in no way looked like a victor but in her opinion clearly commanded the stronger spirit. Now little knives, with which the fatal blow was to be delivered, were fastened to each rooster's right foot, from which the long spur had been removed. A strange quiet prevailed in the round. A professional silence. The cocks apparently showed no interest in measuring their strengths. They acted much more as though they were looking for something edible on the ground dirtied with cigarette butts and other trash, pecked around casually here and there, stretched their heads jerkily, and had time and no hurry, until they surged against one another in an unforeseeable moment when I was distracted by an enshrouded Indian woman with a face with thousandfold wrinkles who was calmly stuffing her pipe. It went quickly and without torture.

Our rooster, which had seemed like a loser, a crumpled little heap of feathers and shrieks, pulled himself together once again, trembling, and with a high leap dealt his thicker, stupefied opponent the fatal blow. I had to support myself on the Indian standing in front of me to see over his head the wounded rooster from whose sliced throat blood appeared in pulsing intervals and at once ebbed. Those standing around now relaxed, money was paid out, palaver began, the owner of the victor shut his plucked charge into a basket, where alone and cramped he could celebrate his survival while his master took a deep drink from the bottle. I was so upset that I urged Luisa not to wait for another fight. A fidgeting unrest, which had been fanned by the strange atmosphere, had gripped me and led to a hysterical wordlessness.

I said nothing more. Heavily gasping, I inhaled the damp air, and kept running a little ahead, pulling the reluctant woman by her hand behind me. When we finally arrived at her house, which now lay quiet and dark in the night air, Luisa, who stood placid and pale before me, looked at me wordlessly and waited for a sign. It was a long time before she concluded her scrutiny, which in part was certainly to be attributed to the circumstance that I, unpracticed in such direct confrontations, nervously stood now on one leg and then the other, wiped the perspiration from my face, and all in all did not correspond to the ideal image of a seducer. I was near the point of putting an end to the situation. But finally, Luisa—at the moment when I was about to break my silence with a word of farewell—pulled me by the hand through the iron-grilled gate, whose hinges screeched as though shrieking, into the parklike garden, and led me around the dark box of the house, whose windows stood open to the night, into the garden brisk with cricket chirps, where invisible from the house, behind a kind of magnolia bush whose sweet-clinging aroma I still remember today, there was a piece of meadow that was to become our bed of love.

Love is perhaps too strong a word for the action that transpired on the dew-wet ground and that was hardly appropriate compensation for the painful anxiety that during our union raged through my unpleasantly white, downright gleaming body. Luisa answered my vigorous movements with curious awkwardness, as though she were about to fall asleep, then suddenly, when finally repose was about to enter my body, burst forth with a cry that in its mixture of anxiety and liberation from anxiety still echoes in me today. She was in her climacteric days, she whispered to me as, anxiously giving ear to the house, we climbed into our clothes. Possibly we would be united in "flesh and blood" forever.

While I was returning on foot to the city, past all the sleeping houses with their few dreary lights, I thought of the possible consequences of that evening. Were I to become a father, I did not want to return to Germany. Like one to whom fate has given a hint, I moved through the streets under the gray granite of the sky, a distracted man from whom everything awkward and superfluous had fallen. The weariness and apprehension that had tortured me in this city had evaporated. A pleasant, cold emptiness filled me.

When without thought I stumbled along one of the old promenades of the city, a dog joined me, having slipped out of the column-wide, open gate of the monastery, and was obviously willing to accept me as its companion. It had a trumpet-shaped head and a coat in clumps as though distemper had affected it. I declared this dog, as comical as it may sound, to be my lifesaver. After a long way on foot I took a seat on a bench, completely exhausted, and the dog lay its muzzle on my knee and looked at me with timorous anxiety and at the same time encouragement, as though it were about to say to me that we were the last two survivors in this city, on this fear-shaken planet. The dog, so it seemed to me, knew everything. It had seen unimaginable filth, sordid poverty; it knew hunger and the deepest abandonment. I needed only to look into its dirty-yellow eyes to give up all illusion, to sense the finality of my solitude. For a moment, which stretched infinitely in my imagination, we were prisoners of an insane system in which no spontaneous feelings and emotions existed, rather only stiffly terrified, mute fraternization in which, in a marvelous contraction of time, the past and the future flowed together in a dark point, in a highly combustible point that any moment, at the slightest movement, could explode. All attempts to give my situation sense, a future, a perspective, shattered in that dog's eyes, which, vaulted over by soft, corroded wrinkles, inspected me quietly. And then it was gone. The dog removed his warm muzzle from my knee with a sigh and trotted away, and in the night that had already become brighter, I found my way into the city.

V

SINCE I no longer write regularly, because the desire has left me to ransack my two years in Brazil time after time in new constellations, after lunch—yogurt, a slice of bread without butter, and a bottle of beer—I customarily sleep for an hour. The sofa is in my library so that I am surrounded by my books, without doubt the largest German collection of travel literature outside of a state library, whose number increases almost daily because now, as before, publishing houses supply me with books to review in the futile hope that I will respond. I pick them up, liberate them from their repulsive plastic wraps, throw away the so-called dust jacket—which promises nothing good as a rule, at least nothing about what the books have to communicate—and, following the singular vanity of one at my age, open the index to look for my name.

If a book does not include an index, it is locked up immediately in the bookcase, where until my death it must stand fast in involuntary proximity to other works. If it does have an index in which my name does not appear, it has a chance to be read, at least in those places that concern my enemies. If my name is mentioned, then it is placed next to the sofa, on the pile of selected works, which then, if it threatens to collapse, is moved en bloc to the cellar, where I have set up a reception room for posterity. Where perception is lacking, it must be made up for by books. One day people will speak gratefully about my love of mankind, because I have without a struggle collected the library of my errors for my enemies.

In actuality, a few years ago after an operation for cataracts I gave up systematic reading, although my eyesight is now much better than in previous years. Sometimes I read the newspaper, but without benefit. Revolution in Germany, power struggle in Russia, the new order in southeast Europe—all of that concerns me no more. Anyone who believed that the old Old World turned upside down would be accompanied by an improvement of mankind must have been a fool. It's going downhill. The development of the species is depressing, the world grows tired, I dare no longer hope for a startling miracle. What was once immutable runs through the sieve of history.

Germans have no talent for politics; I've had to suffer from that for eighty years. Especially repulsive to me is the ridiculous talk about a civilized nation, which always becomes loudest when blatant villainy is committed. We are ruled by a band of pompous sentimentalists who conduct their business in the name of civilization and act as though it actually has to do with civilization. They sell poison gas and with the profits finance the peace movement—that's the foundation of our democracy. Nobody there from whom one would take advice. And always the appeal to the dream of a European situation of unity in which the political, social, cultural, and economic conflicts are suspended in order to delude themselves about their loss of Europe. For Germans dream only that everything in the world looks German, and Englishmen want to have it English. And to the

Swiss everything ought to taste like cheese. Everything screamed to bits, talked to pieces, dreamed to smithereens—that's the situation in which civilization has nothing more to expect. Thank God that the Third World War, which everybody seems to have forgotten, will take place only after my death. But it will take place when the supplies are used up. I am old and rich enough to be able to afford a comfortable pessimism. Reality has vanished and what we perceive as reality is only an ironic transfer sticker that is being held up to a running camera by a politician abandoned by all good German spirits.

I still like to read obituaries, to compare the birth year of the deceased with my birth year, 1910, and I am constantly astonished at what a young age people die. It could have happened to me in 1940 in the jungle, but through the attentiveness of my retinue everything always turned out all right. I could even have landed in a caldron, a privilege that is denied contemporary travelers. Lying on the sofa I occasionally imagine that I'm the oldest person in this city who reads, a crotchety owner of approximately thirty thousand books, recipient of the Federal Service Cross and all kinds of other decorations, all of which hang on the heater on colorful ribbons and produce a whimpering clinking when I go out the door with the windows open.

I have resigned from organizations of authors, no longer visit academies—the Rotary Club carries me only as an inactive member. I no longer take part in podium discussions because the question of power and truth in today's context leaves me cold. Movies do not excite me, the theater moves me no more. I've been able to do without the opera for a long time. Receptions, too, must get by without me, since I once, while inebriated, compared the municipal dignitaries and their company with a tribe of Indians: The faces are mostly ugly, frequently with a stupid expression, with a low, sloping forehead, deeply indented root of the nose. The most noticeable characteristic is the snoutlike mouth that is marked by the deep folds of skin stretching from the nostrils to the corners of the mouth. The chief burgomaster was among those listening in the laughing audience.

If it were not for the postal service, only television would still connect me with the world. I watch a lot of television, mostly without sound so as not to be disturbed by the obtrusiveness of voices while watching the pictures. Pictures were invented because humans supposedly cannot retain what they only hear. Since there is no longer anything worth hearing, we are deluged with pictures, a roaring and turbid storm whose substance has long since blown away.

Until last spring my younger sister occasionally visited me with her husband, ten years her junior, both of whom lost their lives shortly before Easter in a traffic accident. I did not drive to the funeral, gave up all claim to the estate because they owned nothing that could have been useful to me at my age. She had been a teacher, he the director of a primary school, unshakable pedagogues—which always irritated me—who were saddened by their retirement.

Twice a week a housekeeper comes in, a Sudeten German with the usual narrow-minded, radical-right views, but (to make up for that) with solid training in cooking, who takes care of my household and secretly hopes to be the first one to find me dead so that she has unnoticed access to the few articles of value in my house. After the death of my sister she importunately asked several times whether I actually had no more relatives and what would happen to my belongings were I, too, to die. She wrote her telephone number down on small pieces of paper all over the house, so that in the case of

my demise I can still reach her. Supposedly she used to
be a singer and has red hair that she wears loose. When
she bathes me, her hair hangs in front of my eyes, too.

And, finally, twice a week the postman, Mr. Bomplang, visits me; he helps me with my correspondence
and takes care of other smaller tasks, so that workmen
don't have to come into my house. He speaks a Bavarian
dialect, which I hardly understand. From his actions I
can make out what he means, but frequently translate
incorrectly. Then he laughs and explains to me as to a
foreigner what he was about to say.

Once I observed the stubby Mr. Bomplang and the
spindly housekeeper while they were embracing, something that has remained indelibly in my memory because
in the hands of the woman, wriggling on Bomplang's
back, hung my grandfather's gold watch and a feather
duster, while her red hair stood like a shining wreath
about the head of the kissing postal worker, who for his
part is bald and unattractive. Since I did not want to take
this scene for the expression of a frenzied love that had
spontaneously come into being, I assumed they had long
since been in collusion. But that, too, doesn't matter to
me. I can be glad that I can keep them at all with the
biological promise of my speedy death. Old people are

not in demand. As long as the woman bathes me twice a week and, following that, for a little extra money massages me in an open bathrobe, keeps my clothes in good order, and feeds me, she can go on deceiving me and planning for the time after my death. She doesn't know my last will and testament—it would disappoint her.

Besides, in addition, a dog is still living in this house—Stanley, a serious, reflective creature with highly individual habits of which, as far as possible, I must be considerate. I have more or less adopted his ideas of time so as not to nettle the indolent side of his complex character.

So I live alone with a dog. Not to immunize myself against the world, which would be comical at my age, but rather as the consequence and sum of my past. Anyone who has been in the jungle knows the temptation of falling silent. Anyone who has stared into the tropical night sky, into the multitude of stars, needs no other company to determine his own place opposite the eternity of the elements. You wither. You become unsightly. The world withdraws from you; you do not have to beat it to the punch. The catacombs of memory collapse and bury what has constituted a man, and to the extent that his memory has deteriorated, to that extent the world vanishes, too. It is so simple to be alone and to live alone when a dog is nearby. Sometimes I listen to his breathing and imagine the rattling wheeze to be the only straw that connects me with life; but that, too, will pass. Masquerade, erosion, dust. Life leaves with a puff of dust, that's all. The attacks of loneliness under which I used to suffer are past. The bitter resentment that choked me has given way to a deep indifference. The vise of the world has loosened its jaws; soon I will drop.

I lie down on the sofa and pick up the first book in reach. It is Humboldt's *Rediscovery of the New World*, a compilation from the reports about the "Voyage into the Equinoctial Regions of the New Continent," the "Essay on the Political Conditions of the Island of Cuba," and the diaries from his posthumous papers, which were in the German State Library of the former German Democratic Republic in East Berlin and had been drawn upon for the first time to supplement the printed parts under discussion. A beautiful, skillfully edited edition that the editor had sent to me, because in the eastern regions, which had obviously put a prohibition on reading after their merger with the welfare state, they were thrown away or turned into pulp—in Leipzig of all places.

I leaf a bit through the parts of the book that I know

and come upon the place where Humboldt makes the decision toward the end of February 1801 to join the voyage of Captain Bandin. He divides his herbaria into three parts in order not to have to expose them to the hardships of a sea voyage, and discovers later that one part, given to a Franciscan along the way, became a victim of the waves. The insect collection was lost in that manner. For years he has no news of the whereabouts of his diary with all the astronomical observations and all the measures of elevation done with a barometer, until by chance in the library in Philadelphia, already making preparations for his trip home to Europe, he happens upon a reference in the contents of a scientific magazine: "Arrival of the Manuscript of Herr von Humboldt in the House of His Brother in Paris by Way of Spain."

Of course, I immediately think of Himmelfarb, who was able to greet the arrival of his manuscript with a delay of about fifty years, under another name, in a translation. I must read his letter. At once. But when I have with effort gotten my legs onto the floor and am about to stand up, Stanley gives voice to such a mean growl that I let myself sink down again. Siesta must be observed.

I want to keep silent about the dreams that plagued

me. A flood of strange memories, a slackening off, a slowing down. Again and again I returned to my childhood, to the garden in Taucha, to my grandparents, who in my dream looked alike in a puzzling way. I could not tell them apart. They looked like children, and a voice asked me, "Which of the two is your grandfather?" I didn't know. No Paradise—of course not.

VI

ONE TIME we were on our way to locate a cave in the mountains in which, according to the Indians, colorful paintings were to be found. "An Indian had gone hunting in the forest near the cave. A stag sprang out of the cave, which he brought down. In the animal's entrails he found hard, gleaming kernels. He inspected them and found that it was gold." The priest had brought us an Indian, a wizened little man with no teeth, his skin with a yellowish cast, who was to serve as our guide. Since he was a mistrustful fellow, we had to imbibe with him for two days. Only then was this enervated man ready to precede our mules.

Our path led us past lonely villages. We stayed the night with a family whose noses and gums had been caused to rot by a disease, so that they could hardly speak. We had to free from his pain an old man who was no longer right in the head and had in a drunken state embraced a cactus. Only with effort could we evade the request made in a friendly manner to take quarters for the night in a communal house, and every evening, in spite of all our caution, we were so intoxicated that the sand fleas easily took advantage of us. By day the sun burned and the small-leafed trees and cacti that grew up above on the rugged plateau gave no or only meager shade. One's eye fell into disuse in the face of this depressing flatness. After two days I wanted to turn back. The reports by our guide about the distance varied from hour to hour and were formulated so obtusely that even Leo, who sat in his saddle with an impenetrable expression, was uncertain about whether we would ever reach the cave or whether we were being duped by an inspired idiot.

The old man had from the beginning slipped into a

singsong, a monotonous melody that he interrupted only when he slid a new piece off the lump he was chewing under his sonorous tongue. An incomprehensible epic that rose from the twilight of that piteous figure and disappeared again at the moment of its appearance. Sometimes while walking he pointed vaguely into the region or very suddenly at the ground without our being able to notice anything. "Holy places," said Leo, and reined his beast past them.

After three days we reached a settlement in which an Italian merchant found himself living with a harem in the midst of several native families. As the leader of a research group, I had the honor of getting drunk with the dissolute Italian, who, babbling, raved to me about Mussolini, the moral beauty of power, while Leo, the subordinate, found shelter with a medicine woman, who dictated songs and fairy tales into his oilcloth notebook for him. We heard her ghostly, monotonous voice, interspersed by loud salvos of laughter. Apparently she was glad that her glorious cock-and-bull stories were so readily written down.

With thrumming heads we continued on the next morning, now again through a forested area. Sweaty, exhausted, and discouraged, we sat on our tired mules, which stank of offal and the iodine with which we treated the deep wounds on the animals' backs, after we had removed the core of worms. After ten days our food supplies were used up, so the shrunken little man had to go on a monkey hunt. Terrible meat, unappetizing. We had to cut it into small pieces so as not to see what we were eating. There was a moment of such bitter sadness as, with eyes wide against weariness, we were chewing away at the dry monkey meat, that a mean bloodthirstiness awoke in me. But even that had no power left to achieve anything. The Indian preferred the hands and feet of the monkeys and ate the brain as though it were a particular delicacy. Roasted over the fire, the spindle monkeys arguably resembled children. My bloodthirstiness was gone in a second.

I had diarrhea, fever, hallucinations. Occasionally I let my torso sink onto the neck of the animal so as not to fall off. Leo was still sitting upright in his saddle, his face as though frozen stiff. The old man, barefoot, was fit as a fiddle. He kept the insects away from his body with a palm leaf. After two weeks, in a deplorable condition we reach the village near which the cave is supposed to be located. A few strangely gray, worried-looking Indians greet us. In a row behind them stand thick-boned women with broad hips who, in spite of their dirtiness, beam ingenuousness and dignity, a dignity forced by poverty. They own nothing but a few rags, arrows, masks, and baskets. Curiosity least of all. Only when I let myself fall off of my mule, incapable of getting onto my feet, do the persons of rank come nearer and pick me up. They drag me like a downed animal across the village square into one of the huts, heave me onto a hammock, and give me something to eat and to drink. Next to me, in cradles made of bark which are anchored in the roof of the hut, hang small children. They make hardly any sound, do not cry, do not scream, just stare at me. In one corner, on a mat made of palm fronds under a mosquito net, crouches an old woman who speaks to herself softly and monotonously.

I was overcome by fear. It seemed to me an absolute certainty that I was to die in that hammock. Unable to move I suddenly had the feeling of being present at my own funeral. Large, open, festering sores covered my body. My nose, lips, and throat felt so swollen that I could not cry out anymore. It also seemed to me that the voices that came from outside became softer, as though the people did not want to disturb my death agony. I tried to breathe as regularly as I possibly could. And sometime or other I must have fallen asleep.

A man joined me who had spent his sperm in the river. A woman came, bathed in the river, and became pregnant. She gave birth to a boy who was blind and deaf and whose hair hung down long on his back. The man came and asked about the boy, whom he wanted to take with him. But the woman hid the child. Then the man became angry and let the river rise so that the people drowned. Only a few saved themselves in a cave, in which they still live today without having ever seen the sunlight again. Into that cave I went with Leo. The bones of the dead crunched under our boots. We heard the rustling of mice and the snorts of tapirs. About our heads evil spirits whirred like bats. In an illuminated niche a wild boar was dispatched. The liver was wrapped in pale, dry leaves and kept under a stone so that the earth spirits could fetch it without being noticed. Soon we stood in the last room of the very extensive cave. Under a crucified man a naked Indian woman was sitting at a Singer sewing machine sewing together large, bloody scraps of skin. It was my skin. When I looked down at myself, I saw how the skin was peeling precipitately off my flesh.

When I finally awakened, I was lying on the floor of the hut, my head bedded in Leo's lap. He spoke to me as though to a child, in a singsong that I had heard only from the Indians, but he was speaking German. "Soon everything will be past," he murmured. "Soon you'll be at home again, in Leipzig, with your dear Nazis, with Father and Mother, with *Streuselkuchen* and gooseberries." A large group of stupidly staring Indians were standing around behind him, many with fetishes in their hands, others with water containers from which they were sprinkling me, still others with healing wood that they were rubbing together with a scraping noise. While immediately I closed my eyes with shame, they crazily began to celebrate my return from the realm of the dead. A horrible drinking bout followed, in the course of which Leo was celebrated again and again, the medicine man with the healing eyes and the healing voice, and Leo sat, smiling ironically, in the midst of this horrible spectacle, his shoulders slightly bent forward, swaying, and sipping now and then at his cup. "You came within an inch of losing it," he said to me later. "Then the Jews would have been responsible also for the failure of German ethnology."

If I remember correctly, I didn't express my gratitude to him, in order not to make matters even worse.

VII

AFTER we had walked around town together for weeks or separated to get our equipment and the necessary papers for entering the jungle, we finally sat opposite one another in the train that was to take us into the interior of the country. I felt defenseless. I was not overcome by the anxiety of meeting strangers, but rather by the deeper-rooted fear of not being able to handle what was alien. My lack of a talent for life gave me trouble. I knew that I was nothing and had nothing to hope for, however, I still could not make the most of my state. Although the window was open, I suffered from attacks

of suffocation, nausea, and piercing headaches that increased in the course of the trip and also spoiled my taste
for everything. And Leo Himmelfarb opposite me, lying
relaxed on his upholstered seat, smoking, talking, gifted
with unbounded imagination. The longer I watched—
had to watch—the rhetoric of his body, the play of his
hands that accompanied his dreamily sketched chains of
thought, the twitching and twinkling of his face, the more
stonyfaced I became. His enthusiasm and his exuberance
silenced me. Luisa had taken us to the train station and
had remained standing beneath the window of the compartment, chatting interminably and dispensing good advice as though we were setting out on a day-trip. Her
rapturous way of speaking, her mania to say everything
had affected me. I had automatically held out my hand
to her through the window, but Leo had leaned far out
of the window to embrace and kiss her again. While I had
to watch how Leo, a minute before departure, played out
his pattern of seduction, tears came to my eyes. It was
disgusting not to be able to control my emotions, at that
very moment to have to submit to a disintegration, a
breakdown, before their indiscreet eyes.

Later, while the train was moving along through the
suburbs, Leo, who had an unmistakable voyeuristic in-

stinct, spoke quite unconstrained about his relationship with Luisa, as though he wished to test my ability to suffer. Indeed, he even went so far as to want to make a confession to me that would have burst the rules of decency, and I, who could gauge the effect of his words, had to downright forbid him to continue his confession. The disenchantment was complete, which did not lessen my consuming fascination. While the material shell of my body still sat upright, everything inside me imploded.

A fly that the wind had hurled through the window right into my eye tore me from my numbness, and Leo shattered the explosive mood with a laugh. His laughter was a curious mixture of control and excess. It burst loudly out of him and could suddenly cease without a trace of it remaining in his melancholy face.

When we stopped at a small place three hours away from São Paolo, I wanted to get out: Leave the train, take a room in one of the dilapidated hotels next to the train station, stay there. Lie on a squeaking iron bed, listen to the cicadas and the brays of donkeys. Write a letter to Luisa and invite her to this dusty Paradise with its faded colors. Run in the dazzling heat across the burning square to drink coffee in a moldy bar. And Leo would travel as my representative to the Indians, learn their language, measure their heads, collect musical instruments, and all that at the expense of the German Reich. After two years he would look me up here again to hand over to me the results of his research. And, laughing, I would pour him a brandy and say that I would not return to Germany. Take my name, I would say, I don't need it anymore.

I looked at the frayed palm roofs of an Indian settlement, at the stifling filth on the square. Clustering to the north were massive, gold-rimmed, towering clouds that were approaching steadfastly and soon would be rearing before us as black walls. I never in my entire life felt so ridiculous, so painfully out of place. Everybody was staring at me, watching me, how I wiped the sweat from my brow, changed my sitting position, rubbed my eyes. Stares that penetrated the dusty air without effort circled around me and hampered my breathing—destructive stares that without illusion cynically exposed my terrible self-pity.

When I looked up, I saw an ox cart standing on the station platform. The sun-splintered plank bed, over which an uncured ox skin was spread as a roof, rested on yard-high wheels made out of one piece. On the bed lay a shifted coffin, a bare wooden box that was inscribed with a name; next to it stood the driver, who, enveloped in a thick cloud of flies, stared fixedly in our direction. He did not make a single shooing motion, although the insects were sitting on his forehead, ears, and neck; he didn't move at all and made no move to load the coffin. Hitched to the wagon were two oxen whose bones almost stuck through their thoroughly mud-splattered hides. "A death cart," said Leo, "which still has room. The driver has time. His indifference, his stony rumination is the sole reality. There's nothing but timeless twilight in his infinitely empty eyes. Nothing can overcome him, no trifle, no mosquito, no catastrophe. But almost everyone who looks at him is stricken with panic."

Thank God the train chugged on again, but his look remained glued to me, his eyes remained behind the windowpane: staring, motionless, a bit puerile, without pity.

To prepare us, Leo, commenting, interrupting, taking notes, read accounts of travels that originated in the area in which I, too, was to carry out my research. Unappetizing. To prevent a premature birth, the father of the baby washes his hands and the woman drinks the water. If the afterbirth fails to appear, then wood is scratched from the inside of the threshold and the shavings are put into the drink of the woman in labor. If a woman wants to gain the love of a man, she scrapes a piece from her fingernails or cuts up a few hairs to mix in his tobacco. Or she sits naked in a large tin tub with little water and, leaning forward, over her shoulder breaks an egg that runs down her back into the tub. With her hand she takes the egg out of the water and mixes it with the food that is set before the man.

So he read aloud one tale after another, with the intention of making me acquainted with the ideas of the people who were not exactly waiting for me, yet the tales only strengthened my disgust. And when after three endless days of travel we could finally leave the train, when I felt the firm, unaccustomed ground under my feet, I was certain that this journey, which was actually meant to lead me into life, was a mistake.

We stood on the train platform and watched in a stupor how our pieces of luggage were placed next to one another, but it did not even occur to me that it was my equipment that would help me survive the next two years. And if Leo had not appeared suddenly with two helpers who picked up our possessions, I would sometime or other have left the train station without even turning around. But there began a bustle into which I was drawn and at the end of which we again walked next to one another through the city to look for our guides for the last portion of the journey.

VIII

ABOUT FOUR in the afternoon Stanley woke me up because Mr. Bomplang had rung the doorbell. I woke from a dream that in substance and audacity was so banal that I grew afraid and ashamed at the same time. Why does an eighty-year-old man who lives alone become ashamed? Can one never get used to having something ancient inside that crouches, hidden and impalpable, causing one to become red in the face? Why should I be responsible for the banality of my dreams? And why wasn't I ashamed when—which God knows was enough to be ashamed about—I behaved in my dream like a hero, a victor? Dreams should be outlawed.

I was sitting on a gigantic thronelike chair in the middle of a river crawling with crocodiles. In part they were swimming in the brackish, bubbly water and slapping their tails hard against the chair legs, so that my wobbly, high seat tottered; in part they lay motionless together with iguanas and geckos on boulders in the stream, opened their jaws wide, and stared at the sun in whose rays mosquitoes were dancing. No boat far or near, but on the shore were a few naked Indians who were busy building a high pile of wood and singing in chorus their monotonous *"Messe, Messe, Macheriada."* Their intention seemed clear. Especially, a white woman veiled in transparent rags enticed me with unambiguous gestures. Sometimes I thought I recognized my mother, transformed into a foolish Fury. Of all people, my mother, who for years had no longer appeared in my dreams.

First of all, I laid before Bomplang the pile of letters that I had no intention of answering: A lengthy one from the president of the Federal Republic, who congratulated me for the "last adventure in a world shrunken in area"; a telegram from the chancellor, who with many enthusiastic readers in the land of great humanists wished me a long and healthy life; letters from the mayor, the president of the cabinet council, who included my family in his best wishes, from the bishop, who expressly emphasized that my criticism of the missionary stations had led to their improvement, from several university presidents and deans, from the managing director of the Union for Threatened Peoples, from the PEN-Club, and even from the Writers Association, from which I had resigned a few years before because that seemed the only possibility of no longer having the pleasure of its newsletter. "Well, you don't have to read it," the president of all the writers had written me at the time. "Not a single member of our Association reads that newsletter, but please do understand that no one can be a member without being reminded every month that our Association still exists." And the general secretary added his best wishes for my eightieth birthday with the hope that one day I would again join the Association so that I could bring my experiences from the wide world into the comparatively narrow world of the Writers Association. A pious wish. Nobody was interested in books anymore, but the Writers Association kept on growing. Nothing but lyric poets, anemic people. If the tongue of God were a pen. . . Not a single personal letter. No invitation, no joke, no effort, no tender gesture, only stupid stuff on deckle-edge paper. The Red Cross had sent a book about the Red Cross; Dietrich's Fine Foods, a bottle of Biomalt "for a long life."

I gave Mr. Bomplang the official envelope from the Federal Republic president and the telegram from the chancellor, along with all the stamps, then we tied the package up with a string, put a piece of paper with the legend "Finished Correspondence, 80th Birthday" on top, and tossed it behind the still-unopened Herder edition, where after my death it would be found by the trash collectors. All Turks, good-natured Anatolians, who reminded me of Nietzsche with budding mustaches over their upper lips, of a funny routine about Nietzsche presented by the proselytized Reds of the Trash Ballet. Thus spoke Zarathustra, except in this instance he spoke no German.

It was more difficult with regard to the letters that possibly required an answer, such as letters from young colleagues who on the occasion of my round-numbered birthday had picked up my works once more and now found expression for their astonishment about them, how fresh and brand-new they had remained. One of them, whose only book I once reviewed and praised, although line for line it was plagiarized with all the errors of the original, had again and again since my sixtieth birthday written me the same letter with always the same three quotations that he had quite by accident found by renewed leafing through my writings and wished to cite as a sign of my topicality, which would outlast the ages. "Answer?" I asked Bomplang. He wrote him a few sentences on the typewriter, which I signed unread.

And finally the mail from publishers, altogether seventeen letters. Some of them included books as gifts, the so-called latest trends, which went right to Bomplang because after reading the first sentences I didn't want them to show up in my estate; others had sent only announcements with the request for me to check them to my heart's content. Because nothing was there even for Bomplang, they immediately ended up in the wastebasket. The letters were answered cautiously, the announcements not mentioned. A French publisher invited me, should I be in Paris again sometime, which I by no means had in mind to be, to dine in a three-star restaurant. The English publisher, a real lord, felt the urge to want to go duck hunting with me. My German paperback publisher sent me a golden paperback the size of a matchbook, on red satin. Only my chief publisher had shown any sense of humor. Since he could in no way think what he should send me, he had refrained from a gift. We refrained from an answer.

About seven o'clock, when the housekeeper was preparing our meal under Stanley's critical eyes and we had turned on the news—without sound—to be able to follow the final destruction of the world with our own eyes, I dictated the last letter of the day to Bomplang. It went to a Professor Miha in GieBen, whom I had met at a literary colloquium in Berlin after the appearance of my first book, dedicated to Brazilian lyric poetry, and who had at the time promised me to write an article for a loose-leaf lexicon on German contemporary literature which was in preparation for publication. The man, now approaching ninety, had written me with a trembling hand that he had finally composed the first draft of the text, which—I should forgive him—had taken so long because I had not tired of having new books follow my first one, so that he had to read the first again in light of the second, the second again in light of first, and the third, etc., which with more than twenty books and innumerable articles—he really did write *innumerable*—that in addition, because they were dedicated to one theme, were indistinguishable in substance, had led to a "merciless confusion" that only now, in his old age, "already at the portal of death," slowly began to make sense and gave him the justified hope of seeing his article printed in his lifetime—not perhaps in mine—if the lexicon should still exist, which unfortunately was not at all clear. I dictated to Bomplang a missive to the professor, saying that he should take his time with the composition of the final formulation, since both of us, thank God, enjoyed good health. "Today, when everything is subjected to an incomprehensible acceleration," I dictated, "methinks it is reassuring when an article is allowed to undergo a forty-year maturation, and since for some years I have given up presenting my first book in ever-new variations, you may be assured that you will not be forced because of new publications to take up the old stuff again. So you have time," I dictated in closing to my head-shaking corresponding secretary, "and should not let your joy in the labor be taken away from you by exaggerated haste."

Every article that was not written was—like every letter that did not reach me—a welcome relief to me. Given the prevailing laziness of professors who held out for their whole lives unexamined in their positions, it meant on the one hand saving time, since the writers of articles, especially those that turned out positively, had the unpleasant trait of asking countless questions of the object of their reflections—the author—as well as sending countless drafts of their work to be read in turn, an activity that he had to perform carefully in order not to let the positive tendency turn into its opposite. On the other hand, the professors expected from the author an abiding demeanor, an empathetic, stringent course that would not want in any way to get involved with any silly idea, any aberration. They wanted a completed work, not works.

A poet I know, prevented from maintaining a stringent course of life and of work by the heavy blows of fate and the congruent jostling of alcohol, weary of correspondence with professors, had taken matters into his own hands and had himself written all the lexicon articles about him under various pseudonyms, whereby the peculiar circumstance occurred that the most important lyric poet in Germany since Rilke and Benn, according to all the reference books, was completely unknown to the public. To the public! It's a shame to say those words, when talk is of poets.

However it may be, Professor Miha from Gießen can sink safely into his grave without having celebrated properly me and my work. And probably, after opening the letter from Leo Himmelfarb, all the references about me as an author will be rewritten anyway, if they are not completely stricken without being replaced. Remarkably I was not at all shocked at the idea. Something would happen that had to happen sooner or later, and I might even live to see it.

There was bratwurst with potato salad, a dish that no one in the house liked but that was served once a week because Stanley was allowed, in a manner of speaking, to eat with us at the table, although after eating the sausage he had considerable flatulence and with a guilty look broke wind that could not be ignored even during a louder conversation. There was beer with the meal. I remembered how on a river trip in the jungle with Leo I had drunk the last bottle of beer after we had noticed that one of the Indian helmsmen had drunk the box empty down to the last bottle and had steered the pirogue into the bushes on the shore, into thick foliage from which suddenly an arm-thick snake had hissed out at us. "We drank to our good fortune," I said. Bomplang, without a pronounced imagination, listened enthralled as always with his mouth open, the housekeeper made a face and said that everything was a bald-faced lie, and Stanley kept farting softly but clearly audibly.

To have to watch Bomplang while eating was like being tortured. Not only did he place his left arm between the plate and the edge of the table to keep his upper body from preventing his mouth from taking food without making a detour over his place setting at the table, but also, while he was chewing with his mouth open, he propped the elbow of his right arm on the table, whereby the fork that he gripped with all his fingers hovered and seesawed over the table, indecisive about ever reaching the plate again.

The table manners of the natives always had been odious to me—that smacking and grunting, and the indifference with which they stuffed themselves full, the atrocious belches afterwards. Leo had studied these customs lovingly and had written them down, while I could bear them only unsympathetically. He had found pleasure in the role of the observer; it incapacitated me. And while I longed for a proper table in a clean restaurant, he became an ally of those poor devils, who sat half-naked around him without a chance of even imagining a German restaurant. With wide-open eyes they munched on the moldy white bread and listened to his stories, those comedies in which clouds of merriness moved over a peaceful land. Nothing disgusted him. Without his ever having demanded gratitude, they thanked him for his illusionary fairy tales, his stories of survival. I had expected that he would need me to make his misery more bearable, but he seemed to get along without my bolstering brain. For him I was the failure.

In my guilelessness it dawned on me only shortly before our separation, when I still imagined I was leaving that hostile land in triumph, that, in his stinking camp with his face distorted into a caricature, he had actually been the real victor. I didn't want to envisage how that victory looked and whether it was understood by him as such. So I forced myself, resisting my disgust, to look again at Bomplang, who was just then putting the last end of the bratwurst into his open mouth, wiped his mouth with his fork in his hand, and prepared to get up to turn his attention to the rest of the letters. My dislike for this friendly man increased suddenly. I felt the blood shoot into my head and hammer wildly at my temples.

At nine-thirty I locked the front door behind the two of them, got a bottle of red wine from the cellar, went with Stanley into the library, took the letter from Haifa from my desk, and sat down in my armchair, inwardly prepared to find out my verdict.

It could not destroy me. Who would believe a sev-

enty-nine-year-old Leo Himmelfarb from Israel, who re-
primanded an eighty-year-old German writer for having
published his work under a false name? Above all, when
the reprimand comes nearly forty years after the appearance of the book, which is famous all over the world?
There was no proof in strange hands as long as only I
knew about the safe deposit box. In any event, right away
I wanted the next day to rent another safe deposit box in
another bank to keep the key in, since naturally the
danger existed that the housekeeper had long ago ac-
quired some knowledge of all the keys in the house.

I was afraid only of the press. Jealous persons full of
envy among the reviewers had noted in some of my birthday articles that my work had a narrow foundation:
based on the observations of a single journey in the forties, during the time of National Socialism. It was curious
that I had obviously never had the inclination again to
travel through Brazil. One had even written that I would
avoid Brazil in order not to have to correct my perhaps
somewhat naïve image of the Indians, seen from an ideo-
logical viewpoint. And suddenly it seemed to me as
though behind all these hasty remarks the suspicion existed that I had never been to Brazil and had received all
my knowledge secondhand, if not actually plagiarized it.

Himmelfarb

I was already tempted to get out the birthday articles to allay my now intensely seething irritation, but I had forgotten behind which row of books I had stuck the folder. I would ask Bomplang when he brought the mail tomorrow.

I had no choice but to read the letter. Deep inside I fell back to some extent into another situation, into a different world, in which there were still none of the truths that now waited for me. It seemed to me as though I had to pack my suitcases again and leave the fenced-in region in which, in spite of political events, I had spent a normal childhood, to set off into a boundless distance, into a region of decision. And the very uncertainty, the sheer intuition that it would end in defeat drove me away even stronger, until no country, no moral alternative was in sight anymore. Suddenly I was alone, as back then, when except for a few letters of recommendation I had nothing with me. A German university assistant with no experience abroad, who had descended from a civilized world onto the plain of adventure without hope and without any prospect of making something of the situation, and with an expectation in my heart that had nothing to do with life as it was.

I stared at the envelope, at the handwriting so famil-

iar to me in spite of the time that had passed, the stamps
that the postman would receive, the name of the sender.
It was a large, rectangular envelope, light brown in color,
with a pointed flap that in addition was sealed with tape,
as though Himmelfarb had been afraid that its contents
could be scattered on its trip to Germany. Trembling I
pulled the tape off and gave a start at the scraping sound.
Stanley, too, who the whole time had watched me with
his head on his paws, wrinkled his left eyebrow and
sighed. Then, as though in a seizure, I tore the flap open,
irregularly, in such a way that the handwriting became
visible, tugged out the thick sheaf of leaves, smoothed it
over my knee, and read.

IX

*D*EAR RICHARD—

I am sorry to shock you on your eightieth birthday with a sign of life from me, and I can only hope that the Israeli Postal Service is as bad as its reputation, so that you will receive my letter only when all those who congratulate you have left your home again. You do have a home? My German—and for this you must forgive me also—is somewhat rusty, anyway not as fluent as it was fifty years ago, when in spite of my illness I dictated your book to you. My book, to be exact. Back then you could understand my whispers, my feverish words. Probably our language was the only thing binding us together. At any rate, it was the foundation from which our earnestness came. It was the precept. Meanwhile, perhaps with all-too-much comfort, I have spoken other languages and never again reached the linguistic familiarity that prevailed, in spite of all thoughtlessness, between us.

Recently, for the eightieth birthday of the founder of the firm for which I have worked here, I gave a speech in the German language, because all the well-wishers came from Berlin, Leipzig, and Würzburg for the anniversary; old men like me who suddenly had something submissive, something preoccupied, dreamy, reflective, artless about them, a kind of embarrassment in their eyes, a passive, shy smile, until tears came into my eyes. It was a solemn and somehow also lamentable moment, the way the language ate through filth, the stickiness of memory, and became free, but it was, of course, no triumph, for the shameless hope of curing an incurable sickness through language was washed away by the tears, wiped off with the back of my hand. But still, after in the last few years I had become accustomed to speaking almost exclusively English and Hebrew, and the latter still very clumsily, I had once again spoken German.

Himmelfarb

I practice my Romanian occasionally with a neighbor, who is translating Ionesco. I can use Russian almost daily because in my neighborhood a lot of Russians live, all gifted musicians, whole symphony orchestras without a concert hall. I have practically forgotten Portuguese and Spanish, but Polish and Yiddish stay with me.

The language of the aboriginals, however, for the knowledge of which you once admired me, has subsided into the plasmatic tissue of my brain. When just now I read a few crumbs of it in my/your book, something "rang a bell," but so far away that I did not follow the tone further. In short, I am glad to be able to write you this letter in our language, in the language of our book.

Since I will not be alive much longer—I know, I asserted that once before but this time I am quite sure: chronic bronchitis, arthritis, and a few other aches and pains will take care of my leaving this world soon—this letter will not only contribute a few things to clarify our relationship but will also give me the opportunity to get something off my chest. Whatever happens to the soul— and you can imagine that in this land the fiercest speculations about that are being made—if one day, without the protection of the body, it wanders around in this world, then it won't be impaired in its movement by old worries and monstrous phantoms. It will be weightless in the sea of motionlessness.

You can imagine how perplexed I was when I saw a book with your name at the bookstore. Perplexed is the wrong word. I was stricken. Incomprehensibly agitated, I first of all had to leave the store, stormed into a café to get something to drink, and only after a goodly time (by the way, a nice word: goodly) did I go back to the bookstore. It isn't that I had thought constantly about you—I haven't once had serious feelings of vengeance, and in recent years, I gladly admit, I have sometimes even forgotten you, as though we had met in an earlier life, in one come to an end permanently, which had nothing to do with my life in Israel. Sometimes I thought—I don't know why—that you had to be dead, no longer alive. I imagined a tombstone, a few flowers next to it, forget-me-nots, and an old woman sitting on a bench in front of it, guarding your secret. But in that moment, when I read your name, black on white, with my own eyes, my old life crept back into my skin again. I again saw myself lying in the miserable hut, bitten by insects, melted by the heat, and I saw your face before me, your earnest, mistrustful face, your listening attitude—and then I wished you had been dead.

At first I wanted to steal a copy, help myself to it, as

we said in Berlin, because I didn't want to have to pay for my own book, after all. But the bookseller, an American I know well—our firm orders all its books through him, and he has occasionally recommended new books to me, even German ones—was already standing solicitously next to me because he thought I would collapse, keel over in his beautiful store. I wanted to steal a copy because I didn't want to buy a book by you. Finally I did buy it, at a horrendous price because books, especially translations, are incredibly expensive in this country. I have, dear Richard, bought a book by you, a travelogue about the primitive inhabitants of Brazil, appearing in a series of classical travel literature with Richard Byron's Road to Omaha *and Bruce Chatwin's* Songlines; *a paperback book, translated from the German.*

Like a sleepwalker I went home to my apartment— three beautiful, big rooms—and tried to let the painful, bleak reality again penetrate my consciousness. I saw your picture on the back cover; I tried to recognize in the features of the old, chubby man with the bushy eyebrows my friend of more than fifty years ago, the timid ethnologist from Leipzig who had asked me at our first meeting to let my name be omitted in his report if it came to publication, for reasons that I would surely understand, that naturally

I did understand, for you had confessed to me with a laugh that the director of your dissertation had warned you against Jews and Communists. If I were to publish a book about the journey, I would also not have to mention you either—that was our mutual agreement, in the first year of the war.

Well, then I opened up the book. I must even now falter when I think back on that moment. How could you perpetrate that tastelessness, that malicious, vile trick? With bitterness and rage I read the dedication. You had the impudence to dedicate my own book to me: "For Leo Himmelfarb, my faithful companion." My faithful dog would have been more suitable. I cannot and will not say what happened in me when I had to read that dedication in a book that in spite of the translation—an apparently very good translation, by the way—I recognized as my own book, word for word, image for image. You made me, the author, who was forbidden to become a writer, into a porter, into a faithful companion who trotted in your footsteps through the jungle, a coolie and secretary who entertained and cheered you up when the strangely aggressive Indians did not want to tell you how the reckoning of their gods functioned. Didn't anyone ask you who this Leo Himmelfarb is, and whether he was still alive, and where he lived?

Himmelfarb

Did you perhaps, in one of the many books that are listed in your bibliography, report about the death of that Leo Himmelfarb, who was devoured skin and bones by the Indians?

I have neither the time nor the inclination to read your other works, but after this disgraceful dedication I believe you would be capable even of that. I don't believe even today that you were a Nazi when we got to know one another, and whether you became one in the last three years of the war is beyond my ken, but I can very well imagine that after the war you gladly used my Jewish name to make clear once and for all that in the year of the war's beginnings you were not on an official mission.

Since I know that you stole my book, my language— yes, you are a language thief—since I know that in your long life you were capable one day of seizing my sentences and publishing them as your own, since I live to an extent in you, as your author, your writer, as the one who was awarded the honorary doctorates that you possess, as is reported proudly in your biography, since then I must look at you with different eyes. Dwelling in you is awful, dear Richard.

By the way, in your favor, I assume that back then you actually did believe I would die in a few days. I thought no differently myself. Furthermore, I will admit that you were a bit sad to see me dying after everything we had gone through together. And that was more in those two years than normal married couples experience in their entire lives. And finally, still in your favor, you will have thought of me many times on your journey back. I am interested in knowing when you decided to let me die in your mind as well.

Now, there must have been a day when you said to yourself, Now the war is over, it's open season now—like at the sacrificial rite where we were both present—I can eat his soul and publish his manuscript under my name. Why did you wait so long, for instance? What did you do during the last years of the war? Were you drafted? As an ethnologist did you take part in experiments to perfect the Aryan race? Were you busy in a camp? In the one perhaps in which my family was allowed to "live"? Was it painful for you, before 1945, to embody a Galician Jew, whose father raved about the Emperor Franz Joseph and whose mother about Martin Buber? Why did you wait so long? And why didn't you become a professor instead of a so-called free-lance writer? Those are questions that you must answer for me, if you don't want to die of self-loathing—yes, of self-loathing.

Himmelfarb

Please don't get the wrong idea. I don't want the royalties for my book, although the amount produced by all the editions listed on the cover blurb would certainly find good use here. Money doesn't interest me anymore. My apartment belongs to me, I have some money in the bank, I don't want to travel anymore. Close relatives are no longer alive either; they died in one (the German) or another (natural) way. Not even fame appeals to me. The idea that next year for my eightieth birthday, which I may still see, television people from all over the world will show up to interview the true author of a worldwide bestseller about the Brazilian Indians is frightful. Too many crazy people live here anyway, so it's better if you remain inconspicuous. (It just occurs to me that I would have some use after all for the royalties owed me, but never mind: This country won't survive through book royalties.) No, neither the money nor the fame can still excite me in my utmost being. I gave up the dream of becoming a writer after I arrived in Israel (where, by the way, there are some very good writers!), and I would never have dreamed that my poor, fever-bludgeoned book about our journey would become a success.

I can tell you that it fills me with secret pride in my old days to have become a recognized writer after all. My father believed in my talent; my mother prayed it into being; only the Nazis had a different idea. (Can you remember that I told you about a novel that had already been accepted but then could not appear in Germany? Thank God! It was a lunatic fancy of the worst kind, as only a country boy in Berlin could think up! The son of the publisher who back then wanted to publish the book was recently in Israel; a nice man, also a publisher in New York, so there was only a short interruption in their great publishing activity, a small crack, into which my book, my novel, of all things, had to fall.)

But let's go back; I digress—that's old age.

It's a matter of my name! Before you die, you must give me back my name. Spit it out, vomit it up, but give it back to me. I don't want you to take my name with you into the grave, just as I will find my last rest neither in your grave nor in Germany. (Last rest, another nice expression.) You must part from me, forever. The way you do that is all the same to me, if it just happens soon. I don't want to be your faithful companion any longer, your book-dedication Jew. I don't want to feel your gaze on me anymore, never again.

I await your suggestions.

When I heard in Mexico in 1945 what happened to my family, I swore never again to set foot on German soil. It

111

will stay that way. Of course, I would like to have seen Berlin again, today, after the reunification, (which was received here with mixed feelings, which however I personally welcome)—the slums, Skalitzer StraBe, where I once lived—but I will deny myself this more than dubious pleasure. When you've seen too much in your life, at the end you get by with a couple of pictures, with a few memories, in which everything is contained. Travel destroys memories. There was a news item on television—that must suffice. We can meet here, if that does not seem weird to you, or in Athens, or on Cyprus, anywhere halfway. If you don't want to upset your family, tell them you have to introduce your book in Athens or that you are receiving another honorary doctorate in Nicosia—or tell them that you want to meet an old friend from the time in Brazil who is at the point of death and wants to see you once more.

It's urgent, as you can imagine. A letter by express airmail takes about a week.

Waiting for an answer,
Your Leo Himmelfarb.

P.S. Just as I was about to put this letter into the envelope, it occurred to me that I haven't told you a word about the time after our farewell, and although my fingers hurt—I was in the computer business but can't operate a word processor, and you're not here for me to dictate to—I still want to tell you in plain language what happened after your departure:

Only a few days after your—shall I say cowardly? excessively anxious? mean?—departure, the fever subsided. The headman's wife, to whom you ascribed the worst intentions, revealed herself as the real rescuer, for when the men had done all they could and still hung around my bed babbling helplessly, she was finally called, and she left me again only when I could essay my first attempts to walk.

I will spare you with what means she cured me; I still know very well how strongly you could be nauseated; It was horrible. But the real process of healing began when with a pointed bone—a holy bone—she slit open the whitish furrows that had been dug by the insects under my skin. Systematically she opened all the channels, removed eggs and pus, and covered my body, bleeding from a thousand wounds, with healing essences that were prepared under a constant singsong in my presence. The priest, too, who constantly belied his own teachings with bad examples, had long since taken off, naturally to get help, which just as naturally never arrived.

Himmelfarb

After about a month I was restored to health again but stayed on for almost two years. Soon we could get along quite well, and it wouldn't have taken much for me to remain permanently with those people. You see, as thanks for the help that I rendered them after my recovery, they offered me a wife. As a present. In those two years we erected a very respectable village, ran a well-kept farm, even received some subvention from the Church, which soon got wind of our work. They even wanted to send us a new priest, which, to the applause of the Indians, I was able to ward off successfully. I had had enough of theology.

At the end of 'forty-two under a shabby pretext I left the village with a governmental commission, naturally with the assurance that I would soon come back and live with "my present." But I couldn't do it, didn't want to do it anymore. The following years were difficult. I traveled through almost all the countries in South America, mainly as an insurance agent for an English firm, and talked poor people into buying policies. Sometimes in the evening in a cheap hotel room I worked on a story, on a small poem in the German language, but it was all trash, not worth mentioning. The language had something against me, or vice versa. I never married.

In 1953 I came to Palestine, another decision that

lacked all logic. A few years ago, as a co-owner and vice-director of a computer subsidiary of an American company, I retired, sold my share, and got an apartment in which I will live to the end, if the gods that prevail in this region and appear under many names will it so. All the details later. For there are details that will interest you as a writer.

P.P.S. In my life, my crazy, adventurous, banal life, one moment always was lacking: a moment for love, a moment for reflection, a moment for repose, a moment for doing nothing. A moment for me. I'm afraid you are the thief of that moment.

X

STANLEY has worms. So I went to the veterinarian with him, took a seat, which was ridiculous enough, in the terribly decorated waiting room between a woman with a half-dead bird, whose almost bald head hung wearily into the water bowl of its birdcage, and a lady cat owner who talked incessantly to a fat tomcat that, for its part, fixed its gaze with a jaded expression on Stanley. If the noble dog had not shivered constantly, I would have fled at once. An unwarranted premonition. "He will soon die" went through my head, but above all: "He won't let me expose him again to this waiting room, these horrible

116

art prints of animals on the wall, this sourish smell, this linoleum floor with its colorful pattern." And above all, not to the lady doctor, an elderly Miss who with a frightful babble had bent Stanley's tail up to perform her office.

I saw his wrinkled brow, on his left jowl the drop of saliva that stretched out heavy and viscid; heard the whimpering sigh that came out of his unmoving mouth, as though a different animal were within him, hidden in this furry body; felt his indisposition, his hurt dignity; and I felt almost like vomiting with misery because I had brought him this shame. If I ever do have the strength to write something, then it will be the powerful story of the friendship between Stanley and me, a monument of brotherly love that has bound us together for years without doubt, jealousies, or envy.

Some time ago a young woman appeared at my door who wanted to write a doctoral study about me, my work and perhaps also my influence, as she said coquettishly; a comparison of all the numerous studies about the Brazilian Indians that she had already read and could recite to impress me, but whose sole goal consisted of correcting me, reprimanding me for errors and omissions, finding fault with the incorrect dating of masks and emphasizing the fragmentary description of death rituals—a cheeky female who had naturally never been to Brazil. After only two days she had felt at home and begun to make notes for a biographical profile—not academically, but for relaxation, as she put it. She had talked about my mannerisms, about my prejudices and failings, and if I had not thrown her out under a pretext, she would have begun to count my socks, as though in that fashion she would get to the mystery behind my books. The profile was then actually printed, describing a grumbling old man who with the help of his bloodhound kept the world away from his door. She really did call Stanley a bloodhound.

No, Stanley did not deserve to be remembered as a cursory arabesque in the life of a travel author, and when we finally were allowed to leave the veterinarian house of horrors, I swore to him that the following day I wanted to begin writing about our first meeting.

But it never came to that. Was that why Stanley was so irritable? I had hardly read Leo's letter to the end when he let out a howl such as I had never heard from him. Maybe he felt neglected, maybe the birthday turmoil had exasperated him, the steady ringing of the doorbell, the telephone, the flowers whose aromas were unfamiliar to him. He was uneasy, trembled occasionally, got up cumbersomely and lay down again at once, as though there were no reason anymore to step out into the world he knew. "What's the matter with you?" I asked him, with all the sheets of the letter on my lap. He gave a resigned sigh, a long, drawn-out, softly snorting sound, and looked at me with heartbreaking anguish, his brow in thick wrinkles, his eyes wide open. He also opened his mouth to say the decisive sentence, which, however, remained unsaid. It is commonplace that dogs in a shared long life understand a person, but I was suddenly no longer so sure that I had also always understood Stanley correctly. "What did you say?" I asked him, and again there came from his body that sound that was unfamiliar to me; yes, from his body, for this time he had not even opened his mouth.

"Maybe we'll just take another walk," I said, although it was already past midnight. Stanley got up, a procedure that now really worried me. Generally he got onto his feet in seconds, but now he exerted himself with popping joints and hanging ears.

After I had put the letter away in my desk drawer, we walked though the back door out of the house, because I was too lazy to unlock and then again lock the front door. I'm really getting lazy, I thought, since I don't write anymore, lazy and cranky, but also indifferent. Maybe it's the best preparation for death, if you look at things without interest, no longer look at their utility.

We walked past a beer garden where a few customers, who had placed their coasters on top of their glasses, were still sitting. A dog was also present, who somehow seemed forgotten and now began to move toward us, but capitulated before Stanley's sovereign contempt. He was already lying down again on the dirty gravel, his head on his paws. The waiter, a Yugoslav from Sarajevo with whom I sometimes exchange a few words at noon, was standing in his green apron in the door and nodded wearily at me. He had a craving for confidences, since he could not go home again. His children were teased at school. On the small bridge that led over the Eisbach into the English Garden, sitting with bottles of beer were two homeless men over whose outstretched legs we had to climb. "What's your mutt's name, old man?" called out one of them, who had on a red undershirt; then both laughed, but we said nothing and didn't turn around either, rather took the path to the right, along the brook, which led to the art museum.

It suddenly occurred to me that I had never been in

the art museum, so I repeated that sentence aloud to Stanley, who softly lifted his head. I was repelled by the carnival parade of the entertaining arts, the repugnant enthusiasm for pictures by a stylish society that set the tone in this city, all those smiling parasites and geniuses of mediocrity who made use of fascist decorations for their own absurdity, their eyes full of evil goodness when they had themselves photographed. It could be felt how thin the gloss of knowledge and participation was, which only scantily covered the underground of greed and barbarism on which this fine society was erected. "Garbage, not worth mentioning, Stanley," and Stanley snorted to himself in agreement.

Suddenly it was clear to me that we both would die soon. Not a premonition anymore, but a certainty. Maybe the letter had been the release mechanism, because an impetus is always required for one to become familiar with that irrefutable fact. Maybe it was the lamentable attitude of the dog. But suddenly it was certain; the verdict was announced.

I had to sit down on a bench in order to tolerate this new certainty, and I asked Stanley to take a seat next to me. "Nobody's looking," I said to him when I lifted him up next to me because he couldn't manage the height by himself. Now he laid his warm, critical head on my knee; I laid my hand on his head. Before us, reality was shielded by a soft, somber darkness. A bicyclist rode past, with a singing dynamo that gave electricity to a flickering headlight. He looked back at us as though at a pair of lovers.

Should I really go to Cyrus in order finally to part from Leo, as he had suggested? And who will take care of Stanley in the meantime? The housekeeper didn't like the dog because, as she said, she couldn't stand his slobbering. "Let him wipe up his slobber himself," she had snarled recently. Her feeling was naturally mutual, for Stanley could not stand the housekeeper either and left the room deeply insulted when she massaged me. Probably she did not like him because he treated her like air, didn't even raise his head when she reviled him, or broke wind, which put her in a rage, though it made me laugh. I had visited an Indian tribe that, when the harvest was bad, tied their dogs to poles and beat them, so that the evil spirits would be driven off by the howls of pain. But the evil spirit from the Sudetenland was stronger than the old dog. "We could book a voyage by ship, Stanley, travel on the train to Italy, then by ship to Cyprus in a luxury cabin for two persons. Money is no object, for it will definitely be our last trip."

I resolved to reply to Leo to that effect. Now that it was decided, I even felt a kind of joyful excitement rise in me, an inner feeling of agreement with the proposal that seemed but a moment ago absurd. And Stanley, who must have sensed in my hands that something had taken place in me, turned his head to the side so that my hand slid over his ear and down his neck and landed in front of his nose, where he licked it at length and nudged it as though he wanted to thank me for my decision. I will never forget that gesture.

XI

I TRIED to picture Leo as an old man, but I couldn't succeed in drawing a line across fifty years of blank paper from the person I had known into the present. My memory cast a long shadow on my life, in which his own remained invisible. Sometimes I caught a slight, fleet outline of his bent figure, but the physiognomy of an appropriate face did not come. When from the perceptions flitting by something like an expression appeared, they were the features of the young Leo Himmelfarb.

And still, the face that I remembered did not seem identical with the one memory had chained to me. Nothing but superimpositions, double exposures. The figure preserved in me—the eyes, the nose, the stretched-out finger, the emaciated body—was different from the one that now looked at me sadly and scornfully. Memory led me as if by a ring in my nose back and forth between those two faces of that one person until I got dizzy. Just as books read in childhood, which you believe you know in every detail, when re-read seem totally different, at best concur in main characters, so the two Leos sped through my goaded imagination, two young fellows whose paths occasionally crossed but who, in the dark shadow realm of my imagination, never merged.

The part of me that is controlled by my conscience always took the side of the survivor and wanted to see a man who had lived a happy life in spite of everything. The other, more indifferent part that no longer could or wanted to separate out the perceptions, saw a gray, pitiable face that looked confusingly like my own. Like someone who tries to force his forgetfulness by considering his brain as a kind of machine that works for him, I began an inspection of what had been fleetingly preserved in order to find my way back to Leo's true face.

Since Leo's letter reached me, I've been examining my relationship to my surroundings, quite contrary to my custom and also against my better judgment. Up until now I have worked or lazed about, written books, answered letters, given readings and lectures, listened. Everything already had a name that I needed only to repeat in order to make myself understood. And apparently they did understand me. The odd connection between enthusiasm and confused indignation about the course of the world seemed to register. Probably I profited from the fact that an ever more complex exterior life resulted in an inner impoverishment that tended to stupidity, on which my stories of a free adventurousness exerted an attraction.

Even the strange, incomprehensible world of the Indians had become understandable through me. Their different way of life, their myths, their filth—in my depiction the problems disappeared and a strange throng became visible, in whose destiny all the world took part. Every week in a different illustrated periodical a report appeared that asserted in picture and text that these people were still living in the Stone Age. Nonsense, they lived today, probably only today, and tomorrow no longer. But today with impunity you could publish photographs of grinning aboriginals with wobbling breasts, holding cans of cola in their hands.

One day, when animal experiments will be prohibited in Western Europe, they will sew a chip under the scalp of the last Indians in order to save their primitiveness, their inability to be like us. Pigmentation of the skin, the shape of the eyes, strength of character that they lacked—all of that was no longer a problem, given the technology of genetics. The long trail of data on which our life is engraved can be corrected, so why could the Indians not be left artificially at their state of evolution? Then they would not have problems as we do, would not have to struggle with the uses of democracy or the analysis of the internal grammar of a dying civilization. They would be independent of the results of the discussions that are despairingly anticipated at the tables of the West, would not have to look out over the edge of the plate of their own life experiences, and could confidently keep pounding poles into the earth so that the sky would not fall onto their heads. While we rush off toward our end with unexampled speed, they will be left artificially at their beginnings, so that in the next century, too, there can be newspaper articles about them. The quicker the jungle is leveled, the more encompassing their view of us, and then begins imitation, the end.

I myself belong to those who are sluggish. Of course

Himmelfarb

I had taken notice of the world, but I never gave thought as to how it could have been different. The frantic and painful effort to think up a better world and to work on it relentlessly so that such a fancied image would become reality was not for me. With too many sketches of the future, only nightmares had been conjured up instead of visions of redemption. Between me and the world there was no mutuality, no dared challenge. Hopelessly I shuffled behind the era, heard its gasping, its breathlessness, its phlegm, but I would never have gotten the idea to catch up with it, to reach its height. The pinnacle of an era is its downfall. Everyone knows that there are too many of us; everyone senses that cities will collapse, that nature has no future, that our civilization shows signs of infantilism, that the balance between reason and emotion has gone to the devil. Everyone knows, but no one wants it to be true. Only in disguise can life still be endured.

With the insensitivity of a melancholiac I observed my surroundings, society, the world. In spite of the forty-five years since the end of the war I feel no need to arrive in the future, and even today, with death in view, I cannot speed up my thoughts, which were always set to decelerate. Also the fear of being obliterated, which is occasionally present with me, does not concern me really—as a decisive force it is present as an idea but doesn't put fear into my heart. When I thought of death today, I thought of the labor that death brings with it, the terrible difficulties with the bureaucracy, clearing out the house, mail. Nothing else. Actually I have steadily and publicly with success refused to maintain an entry into the world, into its present state, into its Now, and preferred to abandon myself even methodically to forgetfulness. In every respect.

And still there are knocking signals within me that I want to explain. I listen, give ear to the bulging void that demands a name. Suddenly the waste of time, the cheerfully endured boredom, is difficult for me. I want time to open like a book in which I can read; read systematically, to let chimeras and phantasmagoria become reality. But my hope is slight. The listening, the trickling deterioration, the foolish attitude remains. And only when I fall asleep and struggle with the pillow against the aboriginals does something of reality creep into my world, and after I awake, overpowering it, I must hold the pain at bay. But that, too, passes, can be endured.

Today, blown in through the open window, pollen lies on all the furniture and books, a fine, yellow dust. Involuntarily, with my index finger, I drew a line over the dull-looking tabletop that yielded two words: Leo Himmelfarb. Yes, he is here again, even in my hands. That, too, would have to be endured, but additionally came the destructive power of the realization that I had to see him once more. You can't just take off without having seen and touched him once more. And facing him, you must again speak his name aloud, which in his absence comes so easily to your lips. The firm shell of heartlessness begins to crumble. I must, once more, be on my guard.

XII

ONLY DEATH, I had once noted, accepts all stir-
rings, understands them all, endures them all, appeases
them all. I have forgotten who wrote that sentiment,
which has for years been hanging on my desk lamp—now
I can use it.

Stanley is dead. This morning he lay rolled on his
side in his basket. Thank God I was alone in the house
and could take care of everything without having to put
up with the babble of the housekeeper.

I have often been asked why I have spent my whole
life alone, without a wife and without children, without

intimacy, and I always answered evasively. "I have a dog" was usually my answer. Just once in the morning to be nudged by the nose of a dog is enough for the whole day. "I was an only child" was another answer, "and all my life I have been occupied with dismantling the love I received in order to obtain a more direct entry to reality." That was cheating but made an impression. In truth the two years I spent with Leo had been the most intimate years of my adult life, and I draw on them even today. For not only did he "write" me, he also to a certain extent created me. I was his tool. Originally I had looked for someone who was to go into the jungle at my side, but in fact at his side I stumbled into an adventure that I would not have completed without him, perhaps would not even have survived.

Even though I never said it out loud, I was Leo Himmelfarb's student. My flight, aside from the occasion of his illness, was nothing more than the attempt to liberate myself from his influence. But he had already shaped me too profoundly for me to have been able to free myself. I remember very well how, back in Leipzig, I could no longer take the absurd racial theories of my professor seriously. I couldn't even look at him anymore. And if he had forced me—after all, I had been traveling at the expense of the government—to state the reason for my refusal to publish the results of my research, I would have had to tell him that a Galician Jew had opened up my eyes for me, and in the jungle at that, in the company of natives, primitive people on the lowest rung of civilization. An oral examination for my doctorate would have been impossible.

Suddenly I remember how Leo and I once after an orgiastic harvest feast set our chairs in a shallow tributary of a river and sat facing one another, smoking. "I don't think you'll turn into a great ethnologist," Leo had said. "You are too little interested in people. Actually, they disgust you when they catch the big ants in order to drain off their fat. You don't see a broad face that is marked by grave illness, you see an ugly face, burst pustules, gaps between teeth. Everything you see is not another form of what you depict or want to depict, rather a form of degeneracy. You are not the end of the chain, they the beginning; on the contrary: They are the end, ready to vanish again. In your eyes they have no chance in this world, therefore they are interesting for a young man from Leipzig whose professor is a specialist in vanishing races."

I don't know whether he was right, but it was certainly clumsy of him to accuse me in the middle of the jungle of being unfit for my profession. In any event, I never went traveling again later on. All the books that I have published were nurtured from the experience of those two years and from other publications. There was, and there is, enough written. That I was incapable of love was Leo's succinct comment, and when I was about to protest, he asked me to tell him the crucial love story of my life. With mosquitoes swarming around me, I fell into the trap.

"During my student days in Leipzig," I told him, "in addition to ethnology I was studying German literature, a discipline at the center of which Goethe stood. But there was also a professor who had chosen Hölderlin as his god, to whom he paid homage semester after semester, surrounded and assisted by young ladies. He lectured on Tuesdays from four to six—I don't know why I remember that. My head is full of such irrelevant data— old telephone numbers, train connections between Leipzig and Zeitz that I sometimes recite out loud because they seem to me the real framework of my life; on the other hand, I can't remember my present bank account number. In one of the seminars dedicated to Hölderlin, sitting always diagonally in front of me, there was a girl who absorbed my attention more than the 'Hymns' that were being lyrically interpreted at the front, faithfully, as though our life depended on them. The girl certainly knew that she was being watched by me, at least I imagined that I could so concentrate my gaze that she would have to peer at me through her loose hair, which was hanging over her textbook. She always arrived and left alone, wearing a blue, loose-fitting dress and sandals, carrying her notes in a light-blue linen bag. I can remember every detail.

"At the end of the semester, after the last lecture, which consisted exclusively of a reading of all the poems that had been discussed during the term, I walked up to her, nodded, and asked her whether I might invite her for a glass of wine. She had no time. She had to get home quickly, to her aunt, then to the train to go to her parents, who had a farm in the Harz Mountains, mainly sugar beets. Why didn't I come up on the coming weekend, her parents wouldn't mind? She stood facing me in her loose-fitting dress and made me the loveliest offer.

"Of course on Friday I then went up to the Salzgitter region and was most amicably received by the parents and my adored one, to whom in my mind I was already more or less married. I was given a room on the second floor of the roomy guest house, with a view of the placidly sweeping mountains of the Harz and a volume of Hölderlin's poetry on the night table, a dried cornflower between those pages that had one of the—well, the most unfathomable love poems in the German language. I was spoiled with good food, which I was familiar with at home only on holidays, and after the long meal and the cordial conversations about the hardships of living in the country, I strolled with my classmate and her dog through the fields, while the talk was only about Hölderlin, about the love of poetry, and about the sanctity that his verses expressed and poured out. In actuality, it wouldn't have taken much and, having talked, we would have kissed one another into the highest raptures. Anyway we did touch one another's arms to emphasize particular poems and after a long conversation returned as though intoxicated back to the country house. I spent one of the most wistful nights of my life, with Hölderlin, Diotima, the student, and all kinds of other wraiths that haunted my dreams.

"The next morning I was determined to ask the girl's father for his daughter's hand. I walked across the creaking floor to the bathroom in order to take the consequentially important step in a refreshed state. With the foaming toothbrush in my mouth I stepped to the window and was looking lost in thought into the Harz, when I was distracted by an anxious peeping and fluttering from below. There stood my blonde beloved, a blue apron over her blue loose-fitting dress, with a chicken beating its wings in one hand and a small broom in the other, and with its hard end she quickly struck the chicken on the head so as to cut it off with a knife immediately afterwards. As you may imagine, it did not come to an engagement, rather to my departure on the same day. We never saw one another again."

Leo, who had followed my story silently, looked at me sadly. Since he had occupied himself with psychoanalysis and other chitchat, he arrived at daring conclusions that I do not want to repeat here in their distasteful detail. "Anyway, you'll escape marriage in the future, too" were his concluding words. Today I still see myself sitting as though rooted on my chair in the shallow water, as if struck dumb. For deep inside, I knew he was right.

In the quiet of the afternoon, with windows open, I sat down at my desk, took a sheet of paper, one without name and address, from the drawer, and wrote.

137

XIII

D EAR LEO—

Many thanks for your letter, which actually arrived
here a few days after my eightieth birthday, forwarded by
my publisher. I cannot describe to you the feelings that
rose in me at the sight of your handwriting, which I
naturally recognized at once, and I don't know whether
they interest you. At any rate, I was glad that you are still
alive. We can discuss everything with one another when
we see each other soon, as I hope we will.

Forgive the shortness of this letter, but during the night just past my dog died, the only living thing with which I had very close contact in recent years. By the way, he was pleased by my decision to see you, but apparently he was afraid of the long trip, and having to remain behind alone in this house where we live was probably something he couldn't imagine. His name was Stanley. This morning I had him cremated. Too bad that you couldn't get to know him.

For some time I have been living in Munich in proximity to the English Garden, in a small house with a small garden that I have let go to seed. It is my jungle, inhabited by birds. Last year a pair of hoopoes even stayed here, but there are too many cats in the neighbors' houses, so they didn't return.

I have never married. In the fifties I seriously considered looking up a psychologist to acquire some clarity about my decided inclination for being alone, but it remained a consideration. Your assumption that I suffered from castration anxiety scared me more than I wanted to admit. You should have given me more advice instead of terrorizing me.

Then later into my house came Stanley, who could

fill the place of many a human. My cleaning lady, who takes care of household matters for me, will be glad about his death because she couldn't stand the dog's slobbering; she's paid to stand my slobbering. I even think she has hopes for a part of my estate. Anyway, she's teamed up with the postman, who occasionally helps me with my correspondence and replaces my light bulbs. If you live for a long time, you outlive all the light bulbs in the house; technology is weaker than you think.

By the way, Stanley could almost talk. I remember very well the little howler monkey that you kept for a time and that could converse with you, in monkey howls, and I also have not forgotten the ancient parrot, which we could not understand, despite its clear pronunciation, because he squawked to us in an unfamiliar native tongue. In one unfamiliar to *you*. If Stanley had gotten as old as the parrot, he would have survived me, and no one could have understood him.

Munich has remained a small, boring provincial capital in which society is ranked above the individual so that I, who avoid society increasingly, do not exist as a person. Everyone is stamped in the same mold, even the writers and artists, who receive money for doing their juggling tricks. In recent years they were allowed to dance a lot.

Europe is in upheaval, and everyone hopes that now everything will be better. It's getting terrible. Pascal wrote that all human evil came from man's inability to sit still in a room. How true. I once set off, at first alone and then with you, and ever since, misfortune plagues me. Not in a prominent way, for actually I'm getting along well, as well as an eighty-year-old whose sole life companion has died can get along. Also, not least of all thanks to you, I have been successful. Misfortune has soaked the deeper layers, spoiled the foundation, devoured inner stability. No uniformity, nothing essential. I ought to have been decontaminated. Only sheer instinct and laziness have kept me alive. Since Stanley is gone, I know that I, too, will not live very long. So we must meet soon.

I look forward to seeing you again, even if it is difficult for both of us. I would like to make the following suggestion to you: Since it is now too hot to travel in southern countries, I suggest October 15. I will, if you agree, reserve two nice rooms with a terrace at the Hotel Printemps on Corfu, a first-class, old-fashioned hotel with a well-kept garden in which, if it gets too hot inside, we can cool ourselves off. I will book the rooms for one week, but I'm sure the booking can be extended, if necessary, since at that time only a few Englishmen of the old school will be watching the lizards and centipedes that dig their trails under decaying tree trunks.

I'll be coming alone, as I stated, but will bring along a picture of Stanley for you so that you will have an approximate impression of him. (The photograph of the two of us is too large, otherwise I would have enclosed it for you.) I am looking forward to our meeting, even though it will be very hard for me, and not only because I don't want to think about the manner of our final parting: the last word, the very last scene, the final look. Perhaps you still remember how I finally got myself together, climbed onto the donkey, and disappeared. Did I turn around and wave to you? Just as sunken cities seen from above show on the earth's surface the outline of their buildings, as we saw together in the jungle, so a certain imprint that I have received of you will remain visible to me until I die. That means you must survive me; no other possibility occurs to me.

Everything else, then, later, when we talk. In the coming twelve weeks, until our first meeting after almost fifty years, I have a lot to do, which weighs on me all the more because recently I have been really lazy. Not that I'm letting myself go; on the contrary, I have merely reduced all my activities to a minimum. For example, I no longer write. Recently there was an article in the newspaper here stating that authors had become uninteresting. They were just a medium lending their fountain pens incidentally to words flying around so that they would land on paper. At the very instant they are there in black and white, the authors can take their leave, for the sentences no longer belong to them. Whenever they have the inclination, they can hold their pens in the wind again and wait for a few words for a poem to come—if not, then not. Human beings have gone crazy. There are thories everywhere that they actually no longer exist. Only here and there a couple of pens held high in the air, and behind them an industry gone mad that reproduces coincidence and markets it. I want to have nothing more to do with that.

Did you ever see Luisa again? Since here in Germany people occupy themselves with occultism as well as with their theoretical removal, I always hoped to find her name on one of these exquisitely packaged books—alas, in vain. Probably she married a general who lost his life in one of the many putsches and now is using up his pension.

So, until soon,

Your old Richard

P.S. Send me news by telephone whether you can accept my offer. If not, then we will have to correspond again.

I shed a few tears without really knowing what was happening to me. They were running down my cheeks, leaving behind a slight tickle on my skin. When did I cry last? Not that the belated shame about a long-forgotten episode of my life stimulated my tear ducts; I just suddenly felt how my lack of clarity in respect to my own past rebelled against me, and since I was not able to resist that feeling that threatened to take my breath away, vehemently and brutally rushing upon me, I simply avoided it. Perhaps authorized sentimentality will succeed in untying the knot. Sooner or later, but in any case very shortly, physical death will liberate me from such tortures that are fittingly called pangs of conscience. But the uncertainty in regard to the time I still have to live makes it appear advisable to think of other possibilities of exoneration. So I was grateful that my tears, drop by drop, flowed into my collar. Like an astonished child I sat in my armchair, a weeping old man, and let it happen.

XIV

DID LEO still smoke? When in the evening after work we rested in our hammocks, I stuffed my pipe with carefully guarded English tobacco while Leo smoked just about anything the Indians offered him if it looked like tobacco from a distance. Often he choked and coughed so miserably that I feared for his life, but he recovered quickly, lay gasping in the hammock, and raved about the sky. He smoked and read a lot.

Concerning my vexation at the long sentences of Thomas Mann—except for works in my discipline I had only books by Mann and Eulenburg along, which I had bought in an antiquarian bookstore in São Paolo from a German Jew—Leo had only ironic remarks.

"A petit bourgeois puffed up into a bourgeois" was his comment. "Not suitable for the jungle. The idea that you can teach the Indians our language and to read, so that they can study Thomas Mann in the original, is repulsive," he railed in his hammock. "Teach them Ringelnatz or Morgenstern, then they'll at least have something to laugh at when they think back on us."

"Well, he's not a Jew anyway," I said then, insulted, although even here I was not sure.

He liked best to talk about a writer named Paul Scheerbart, whom I long took for an invention by him, because the verses in their screwball silliness that he quoted could only have grown in his manure. If an Indian started something that went against Leo's grain, he said, "Character is mere obstinacy. Long live the gypsy woman," and he split his sides laughing about that adage. But how he could consider those foolish little verses to be more important than the masterworks of Thomas Mann remained his secret. "One day you'll understand," he then said, enveloped in his clouds of smoke. He himself had only Frenchmen in his box of books, the heaviest piece of luggage in our equipment.

Stendhal, Renard, Amiel, Valéry and, added to that, volumes of poetry and philosophical writings en masse. Whenever the Indians put a stronger drug in his tobacco, he walked around the place with his hands raised to the heavens, loudly declaiming, to the entertainment of all the people and animals who had previously never heard anything about Mallarmé. He was possessed. When the effects wore off, he rolled himself into a ball on his bed and fell silent; not even food could interest him then. "Chewing makes you tired" were usually his last words before falling asleep.

XV

IN THE SIXTIES, when my first book appeared in America—a rare success for a German author of travel books—with all the stirring and tedious attendant phenomena, I received a letter from a Russian stranded in New York who asked me about the whereabouts of Leo Himmelfarb, to whom my book was dedicated also in its American translation. At first I had answered guardedly that as far as I knew he had remained in Brazil and probably died in the meanwhile, because all my efforts to find out his place of sojourn had failed. But I was pressured by my uninvited correspondent little by little to communicate further details about Leo, who presumably had been a friend of the Russian.

They had fought on the side of the International Brigade in the Spanish Civil War, had both gotten out with their lives, and had seen one another for the last time in 1938 in Paris in a hotel near the Boulevard Malesherbes, a kind of temporary lodging where Leo was supposed to have lived with his wife and his child. "With his wife, with his child?" I had asked in return and had already become deeply involved in a subject that I wanted to have nothing to do with for very good reasons. But Vassily Fyodorovitch Tchernytch would not be deterred by my reserved taciturnity; rather he piled up further question upon question, and with his thin, angular handwriting spread out before me a whole panorama of a life that could hardly be reconciled at any point with my knowledge about Leo. A case of mistaken identity? In any event, Leo had never spoken to me about his action in Spain, not to mention a family. He had stepped into my life out of the jungle of houses and remained one day in the jungle, a not particularly loquacious but linguistically gifted companion of an episode in my life who had neglected to inform me about his past. Now he was said to have fought in Spain as a young man, on the Communist side; now he had a wife and—what weighed most heavily on me—a child. And soon I was to be allowed to discover that it was a girl who, if Vassily—who always opened his letters with the salutation "Dear Friend"— remembered correctly, was called Sarah.

The power of memory of the Russian, who finally visited me because he had found a position with Radio Free Europe in Munich, functioned excellently. So it was Sarah, who now must be thirty years old. By way of my French publisher I had a search done in the Parisian telephone books and other large French cities for a Sarah Himmelfarb, but, thank goodness, without success. Probably she had married. And probably her mother had also married again. In any case, the Russian left me alone after we had met a few times and exchanged information. Some years later he was found murdered, without the circumstances that led to his death ever being cleared up.

I could remember Vassily very well. He had been a stocky, fairly fat man with soft, gray, somewhat protruding eyes, an embittered intellectual of the sort who suddenly seek their salvation in the reading of poems (and never find it) after they have given up believing in the Absolute. *A God that failed.* He had an intelligence that could never be lulled, although he could never use it for his stupid work in the radio's archives. He continually talked about his early productive work in the Party, which had finally sent him to Spain, where he was at the mercy of lice, hunger, and the sun, uncompromisingly obligated to the thought of the victory of Communism—until Leo had come into his life, the Galician Jew with the broad shoulders and the concave chest who, after the unrest in Barcelona, had opened his, Vassily's, eyes to the Soviet terror and the moral prestige of democracy, which had been abused forever by the Moscow trials. "The dishonor of the Revolution has taken place," Leo had said, when finally they had made their way over the Pyrenees, where on the French side they had been looted by the *gardes mobiles* and stuck in a prison camp—Leo, the scornful clairvoyant, and Vassily, the intimidated renegade. Later, their flight, mostly on foot, through all of France to Paris. In Paris they had parted. "Until later sometime," Leo is said to have called out from the entrance of his hotel, his daughter in his arms. "We'll meet again when the war in Europe, which will start tomorrow, is over."

So Vassily Fyodorovitch Tchernytch, the comical gnome, ended his description of Leo. And in farewell, already on the street that, as I suddenly remember, was wet with rain after a heavy summer storm, he had stepped up very close to me, had with both hands gripped my right hand, and whispered, "Don't get me wrong, dear friend, but I sometimes think you killed Leo."

XVI

SINCE THE ARRIVAL of Leo's letter I have begun to think a lot about our first camp. It consisted of two large, round houses in which lived several families who had followed us from the city, about twenty huts of the natives, who had been living there for some time, and an eccentric building that represented my official residence. Between the houses stretched an open square where the Indians dried the cassava meal on mats. Right behind our settlement the crowns of the gigantic trees closed together high above and formed a twilight space in which the laws of the jungle existed. Between the two realms mediated the Indians who, still chattering on the thin plank benches, had just debated their politics and in the next instant were changed in the twilight and swallowed by the earth.

Since it was my first sojourn in the jungle, my senses needed some time to adjust. So at first I sat as though paralyzed on the wooden steps of my house and stared absentmindedly into the confusion around me. In all that throng there was no pattern for the eye so that only by staring, by spellbound timidity, could it avoid collapse. I saw everything but perceived nothing and could distinguish nothing. The discerner was Leo. He attended to man and beast, had plants gathered that mosquitoes didn't like, supervised the construction of houses, and was occupied with the layout of the garden that he had earlier put down in drawings. He safeguarded our supplies and saw to it that in the evening the implements were in their places again. Neither the noise nor the filth nor the people seemed to bother him.

After a few days he was already living on this godforsaken spot in the jungle as though fate had chosen him for it. He was the converter. He made a suggestion or with his long middle finger drew on the ground, and instantly something was changed. Of course, in the wink of an eye he could come to terms with the natives, who toward me were somber, taciturn, brooding, and in a certain dignified way brusque. Toward him they were cheerful, loquacious, and trusting, which only increased my hate for the people whose fervor soon overlaid my bristling depression. From the very first moment, I was superfluous, and the more I became aware of this feeling, this certainty, the more intensively did I try to wield my power, to which Leo, in the final analysis, owed his existence. But without his authority, my power was pointless.

With Leo I had established four different camps, lived with him in the vicinity of four tribes whose behavior could not be compared. Leo had learned four languages and tried to teach them to me. And even though in the end the total breakdown I feared for our precarious relationship had not occurred, still I never lost the feeling of not being taken seriously by him. In his view I was always the German student, the disastrous result of academic training, incapable of adjusting to strange surroundings, a powerless character who respected what was pure because he was afraid of anything mixed. And really, the mixture of whites and blacks, whites and Indians, Indians and blacks, which I could see before my eyes, gave me anything but pleasure, not least because I did not understand it. But I had to understand something in order to write a dissertation. No dissertation director would be able to force me to love this tangled mixture, as Leo obviously planned to do, and my work could easily exhibit a few paranoid specks of resistance, but a minimum of cognitive, participatory observation was required to be able to get something onto paper. However, since I could summon up no energy to rebuff the destructive insinuations, it was suddenly clear that Leo should also keep the diary.

He wrote, I read and made a senseless check mark under the text, as the last sign of a power long-since dissolved. It was supposed to mean okay, examined and found good. I never had to suggest corrections. So Leo not only saved my life—for without him, as was quite clear after only a few weeks, I would have perished in the jungle, vanished—he also produced the writing on which my entire later existence was to depend. He also lived for me the part of me that was condemned to do nothing. Even now, as I write this report, my hands tremble when I must admit that Leo is still a part of me, my worn-out hands that can no longer really grip anything, these flabby talons with the knotty lumps over the joints, their skin no longer tight.

Himmelfarb

And now our second settlement rises in my memory.
Before me I see the thick green wall of bushes with the
countless little stars that flare up once more in the last
rays of the sun and then close the fantastic philodendron
with its giant heart-shaped, arrowlike leaves, which
throngs around the thicker tree limbs and displays countless thin aerial roots that like cords hang down next to
one another by the hundreds and, with the lianes spread
in all directions through the air or suspended in loose
coils, form a tangled system of cords and rope ladders in
which the crazy, screaming, screeching, and chattering
birds hop around; the odd, chalklike bark of the tall tree
with the umbrella-shaped crown of the most delicate mi-
mosa leaves that stood next to my residence; the large,
silk-blue moth that fluttered with serene flaps of its wings
out of the gloom of the forest and set down in our vegetable garden, which Leo, together with the Indians, had
developed into a place for sightseeing and gaping astonishment famous in the whole district.

In that garden he had harvested fruits the size of a
goose egg, at first green, later yellow in color, whose
insides contained a host of small seeds that lay embedded
in a cell-like, gray-green substance whose taste was remi-
niscent of strawberries. Other more mealy fruits in all

colors and shapes were cooked into a puree by him and spread on flat cakes. In addition he raised beans, cucumbers, squash, and all kinds of pepper plants that lent savor to our food. And, finally, he had taught the Indians how they should manage the maize crops that were cultivated on the fields all around the houses so that they would get decent harvests. Leo, the Jewish writer from Galicia, was the ideal gardener.

In the evening he lay in his hammock and surveyed his work, the inconceivable wealth, abundance, and plenty; while the foremen squatting next to him on the ground discussed the next day; wrote and read and acted altogether like someone who had long since given up Europe in order to live forever in this Paradise coaxed from the wilderness. While I, escaped from the university in Leipzig and the German army, was supposed to enjoy the freedom that I was no match for, and while I was constantly on the watch for principles of rank so I could control my relationship to the people and to nature, Leo followed the principle of taking and giving, of learning and teaching, of listening and storytelling, in a word: of reciprocity, which I could not even imitate. The natives went to him; they were scared of me. And he went to them, queried them, had them tell their stories and explain their objects. They took him along when on days when they had nothing to do they went hunting or visited their tribe. He was permitted to be present at weddings and funerals. He was doctor, judge, and teacher in one person.

At night we sat by the light of a kerosene lamp for another hour on our veranda, Leo with the journal before him. If the day had brought few incidents that were worth writing down, he made thematic summaries, perhaps about cleanliness. Sometimes I had to laugh about those people, for example when with solemn earnestness he described the practice of personal hygiene of our Indians that was lacking. He kept inventing new words to put the unclean, unkempt outward appearance of those people in a better light. Tenderly he recorded that they were housed in smoke-blackened, fume-filled, evil-smelling huts bursting with refuse.

When their skin itched from insect bites, they reached for a gray, greasy clay, stirred it with water or saliva into a thick paste, and smeared it on the itching spot. Near the fire this layer slowly dried and finally was rubbed off again as a fine powder. Leo described this cleansing, which was often enough the only one they took great pains to perform, as though an important step in the history of hygiene were involved. Even for the natives' head hair that was crawling with vermin he found corresponding formulations. It was solicitous compassion when a mother picked blackish lice from the heads of her children and squashed them between her teeth; he described it as an act of consideration when in the evening these people sat with indescribable patience just scratching their heads and picking more and more little creatures from their skin and pitching them into the fire. Everything a family owned was tossed in disorder into a bast basket, where it remained wadded up and wildly tossed about. If someone needed something, the whole tangle was pulled apart and the disorder thus even increased. My well-intentioned attempts to persuade them to put away their articles of clothing well-arranged and folded, to dry them or to clean them, to hang them up and to air them out to rid them of the clinging bad smell came to naught. Things that I gave them they treasured as curiosities for a few hours, then they landed heedlessly in the dirt. Even in regard to this indifferent behavior toward things that represented their only possessions Leo was able to extract a good side, as you can read in my book. He compared it to our concept of property, our rapacity, our decadence, whereby he not only attained a revaluation of the Indians but also produced for me the reputation of a bitter critic of civilization, which provided me with a high distinction among young intellectuals.

When the writing task was completed and the oilcloth notebook stored in a wooden box with lock and key, he returned with a lighted pipe and a big glass of alcohol, lounged in a corner of the veranda, and with me gazed into the night that was shot through with solitary shrill bird cries. The moon slid from one dark pocket of cloud into the next and dully illuminated the objects that we had collected for scientific purposes: food baskets, pots, earthen pans, sieves, mats, mortars, masks, pounders, and calabashes. From the ceiling dangled fetishes, arrows, and stone axes, and in the corners were piled smaller utensils, little baskets and drinking cups, and pieces of jewelry. And between all these objects that were waiting to be described, the ants wended their way day and night, loaded with bits of straw, pieces of charcoal or cornmeal.

It was the hour before midnight when Leo occasionally turned to me and spoke with me. He always began the conversation on familiar territory by telling me what he wanted to do the following day. In order to study the

social forms of organization he wanted to conduct inter-
views among the tribes that lived in surrounding areas. I
was not familiar with those kinds of methods of investigation, and besides I was dubious that even one of the
Indians would ever tell the truth. The net of false views,
bad habits, and evil dispositions was woven so tightly
that there remained little place for truth. But none of my
objections could put off Leo.

In order to arrive at a more exact insight into the
family structure, with me and one Indian he wanted to
spend a few days looking up a tribe that had been com-
mended to him as particularly rich in tradition. He was
insistent that I should come with him. He would not
brook any objection. I had to follow him, do as he did,
otherwise I might possibly be driven out of our camp.

If business was discussed, it wasn't long until he had
succeeded in bending the conversation into a direction
that led without fail to Germany. If during the day he
was a jungle man who managed and kept in order an
impressive camp, in the nocturnal witching hour he
changed back into a concerned, suffering, desperate
European who with his rambling talk brought confusion
into the order and stability of my forlornness, which was
walled-in by fear. In doing so he made no allowance for

my not being a Jew; on the contrary, he angrily confronted me, so to speak, with his Jewishness and challenged me to express my view. I wanted to refuse, but he stuck stubbornly to his questions. And when I cautiously stated that this circumstance would be brought into balance somehow, then he laughed with unpleasant loudness in the humming night. I felt then that someone might be listening to us. "Any further hope is self-deception," he yelled at me, something he knew from the beginning of the new regime, the chief writings of which he had read, of course, though they were totally unknown to me. I had to admit that I knew nothing. He forced me to confess that I had no notion. When the glass of alcohol in his hand was empty and—the mosquito net over his head—he got up to fill it for the last time, he sometimes remained standing before me, swaying slightly, and looked at me, the ignorant one, scornfully for so long that I had to admit I was not interested in certain things for reasons of my own.

If I was lucky, he did not return but lay down on his bed and went right to sleep—also a trait that I admired in him. But this abandonment was often even more painful than his aggressiveness. As long as I was sitting with him on the terrace and was laid siege to by the same mosquitoes, bees, and mutuka flies, as long as he could reconcile his dignity even to take notice of me and to listen to me, as long as that one night surrounded us with its staring eyes, then nothing life-threatening could happen to me. I was safe even in his rejection. Did he have any idea about the power he had over me? He knew it; he must have known it.

When the next morning I tried to remember what we had talked about during the night, he was already out and away. So I had to sit alone in the shade with a heavy head, the financial backer who has no say and watches the people going about their work. I myself owned nothing that I could love. My books? Nature? Science? In the air there lay constantly an odor of overripe fruit that deepened my morning melancholy even more. Like an animal I peered through the bead curtain that separated the so-called bedroom from the terrace. Leo was the village founder who knew instinctively that with his law he had to confront the oblivious jungle, in which there was no road, no monument, no center. His law was the garden, the enclosure, the assembly of the extreme prerequisites for life at a single point, the various foods that were eaten with one another, the variety of clothing, time slowed down, memory, and ways of storytelling.

Himmelfarb

Had we had time, then Leo would have been the founder of a city, a hero in a godless time, who would have loosened the tongue of the jungle and made it speak. "We must make sure of its pronouncements because that is the only possibility of organizing our present existence," he announced to me. But before it could come to that, we already had to pack up again and leave our farm, Leo's farm, to the voracious wilderness.

All of that I saw before me when in the morning, in a safe position behind the curtain, I looked at the busy bustling in our settlement. But my life at the time was not directed toward questioning, because I was blind to social truths. Envy was seething in me and preventing me from experiencing unexpected beauty. Pessimism and fatalism, the unholy duo, governed the course of my day. Once a German priest from the closest mission visited us who observed our curious family with horror. Abruptly he uttered the opinion that the Negro flourished best and felt most comfortable when he stood in a subservient relationship to whites. When he was treated amicably, he recognized without hate the superiority of the whites and acquiesced without grumbling to the modest place that nature had chosen for him on the ladder of her creatures. We were sitting on the veranda and were served by two blacks from his following. When he continued and said that the Negro was as faithful as a dog, Leo sprang up from the table and left the house cursing. But I was not capable of stopping or reversing the priest's flow of words, because that man of God was obviously happy to be able to preach his views in all their scope in the German language.

"Since ancient times," he continued after Leo's departure, "we have seen the black African tribes coming into contact with all civilized peoples one after the other, but we have always encountered their members in the same position in life as slaves and servants. The example of the more advanced nations never heartened them for emulation, rather left them for centuries in the same state of crudeness. The black race," and he closed that part of his lecture, "was inaccessible to civilization in its unmixed condition."

Even today I see his protruding eyes that fixed me over the rim of his schnapps glass, his smacking lips, and the coarse hands with which he emphasized his words. And I still feel today my inability to cut him short, because I was forced to think of my Leipzig teacher who represented very similar teachings. The tongue of the Negro is too thick to articulate civilized languages, but they always open their mouths wide, scream, yell, and are hardly capable of speaking softly. The Indian, on the other hand, timid anyway, gloomy and taciturn, seldom raises his voice and always speaks with lips pressed tightly together. But he didn't have a good word to say about the Europeans either, as far as I could understand him—in any event, for reasons having to do with race, they were in no position to civilize South America. They sweated too much, he had proclaimed to me in his carping Swabian accent, so were to be used only as masters. A new race was required for this region, a race that possessed physical strength of resistance and mental alertness, and the Negro was qualified for the physical strength.

He was born in Treichtlingen, had studied history in addition to theology, and had written a so-called standard work about the Inquisition, which he just happened to have with him and lent to me to read. So then, along with his blubbering commentaries, I could read how the Holy Roman Church had nourished its children, quite without the admixture of the weeds of various errors that have damaged and infected the major part of Europe to our own day. He recommended that I study especially the examples from Brazil, where torture had been practiced most mercilessly. To force confessions either a block and tackle was used, by means of which the accused was hauled up to the ceiling of the room, where heavy weights were hung from his feet; or with hands and feet tied he was stretched over a bench and water was poured continuously onto him; or his feet were locked into a rack, grease spread on their soles, and a brazier put beneath them.

In Brazil, for humanitarian reasons, torture could last only an hour, he added excitedly; in other countries an extension was possible. *Christi nomine invocato*: The judgment was spoken. If the person concerned was guilty, there was an auto-da-fé, an occasion with horrifying pomp, at which the worldly and the spiritual leadership presided and the multitude could be present. My interest was awakened particularly by one case, where a famous theologian had asserted that the Roman Church had fallen into revolting abuses, that the Indians were the true people of Israel, that confession had to be abolished, and that priests should finally be allowed to marry. He was burned to death.

For the three days that our priest remained with us, Leo did not show himself in the camp, which caused unrest that even the Swabian did not miss. I explained his absence by a long-planned hunting excursion, which was embarrassing because at that moment, when the man of God was finally seated on his mule, Leo stepped out of the bushes without any hunting equipment and gave the animal such a slap that the rider was forced to leave the camp in a panicked gallop in a precariously awkward position. "Did you talk to him about me?" he asked me. And when for some reason or another I hesitated, he said, "If you ever tell a white man, especially a German, who I am and where I come from, you'll never see me again." His big yellow dog, which had been given to him by an Indian for a bottle of schnapps, lay with outstretched head and paws between us and for a second raised his right eyelid as though to see whether I had understood correctly. I had understood.

It was no problem to sell my house. Everybody wanted to live in a house on the English Garden. I called my tax adviser to ask him about a suitable real estate agent and heard to my mistrustful joy that he wanted to take over the matter himself immediately "for half the real estate fee and double the trust," as he expressed it. So on the days that the housekeeper did not come I had the pleasure of being allowed to admire the procession of those parts of society to whom the expenditure of almost two million marks caused no headaches. Lawyers' wives who drove up almost nude in convertibles, doctors, sales representatives, tax examiners, all the flies that had enriched themselves on society's cheese buzzed with knowing expressions through my house, complimented the old man who had taken such good care of it, knocked on the walls, and stared with dread directly at the Indian masks that hung at eye level everywhere on the walls. It was repulsive. And behind the decked-out clientele my tax adviser fawned, praised the inexpensiveness of the "thing," and winked at me conspiratorially behind the backs of the people. A man from the cinema asked to see the cellar, whether there were stocks of wine for sale, and I promised to think about it.

Finally I sold the house, against the wishes of the tax adviser, at a moderate price to a young married couple. He was a professor of aesthetics, a repulsive guy, who passed by my library with hardly disguised disgust. He read no "primary literature," as he confessed to me candidly, because it could confuse his theory, only "secondary," but plenty of that, as his wife added, who had sold her paternal pharmacy in Holstein along with the house and property in order to enable the aesthetician who was hostile to literature to live a pleasant life as a researcher with the money. I hope she arranged the contracts so that, after his imminent departure from the house, which I expected, she could at least continue living in my house. The fact that the woman was the only person among the numerous buying customers who had stopped at Stanley's picture was the decisive thing that led to my selling the house to just this unlikely pair. "What a splendid animal," she had said.

Since the aesthetician did not even want the books that were not going to the library as a gift, I had to sell them, too. I put a small collection aside for Bomplang; the rest were appraised and were to be picked up in the second half of October for at least three-hundred-thousand marks, because the old books with hand-colored charts had a good chance at auction to reach a multiple of the sales price. I was a rich man. I bequeathed the masks to the Ethnological Museum.

It was not simple to keep secret from the house-keeper and Bomplang these manifold and in part extensive activities, so in the middle of September I decided to send the woman on vacation for a month. "Go visit your old homeland," I advised her, who at the end of the war had been a year old and hadn't the least idea where the Sudetenland actually was. For traditional reasons she was reactionary—that was the whole nationalistic secret. I paid for her trip and lodging, as well as for the expenses of her mother, from whom I received thanks for that "human gesture in a heartless age" in a letter that dripped at the same time with sheer embarrassment. Now the apartment became noticeably grimy, but I had one less witness.

I felt I was being watched by my neighbor, a newspaper publisher in retirement, five years younger than I, who lived alone in his enormous house, cared for by servants. In the twenty years we were neighbors he had confessed his adventurous love life over the garden fence in installments, a trashy novel that he loved idolatrously, more than the women, of course, who appeared in that comedy. A successful poseur—and because in his newspaper nice things had often been reported about me, I felt obliged to be polite when he wanted to entrust a new chapter of his memoirs to me. After his wife had moved out, about four years previously, he sought my companionship more and more often because, in his words, "We should stick together in our misfortune," an expression that in the mouth of that man, who was excessively callous, had a comical effect.

Whenever he noticed that there was movement in my household, he stood almost daily at the garden fence in his dark suit, a whiskey glass in his hand, and called me over the instant he caught sight of me to reveal further details about his disastrous conduct. His next-to-last wife, the real reason for his amours, a clever woman versed in life, had at a specific time of their life together, when a fairly young female editor moved into the top floor, sued for divorce and had gone her way with a considerable pile of money, so that the neighbor, without this excuse, was forced to acquiesce to the marriage denied to the lady editor by reference to his wife. Without warning he had to marry again, although, God knows, he had not planned on that, and indeed with a celebration that lasted for three days, excessively straining my neighborly patience, at the end of which ultimately the young lady editor owned twenty percent of the publishing house. In celebration of this windfall with the literary editor of the newspaper she began a relationship that both of them enjoyed exhaustively and for a long time, to the delight of the competition, until my neighbor decided upon my urging over the garden fence to see his second wife only at the board meetings of his publishing house. "If you leave, too," said the man who had entry to the best circles in the city but obviously thought a lot of our friendship, "then I can put a bullet in my head and put an end to a miserable life." 'We're too old for promises," I answered this comedian of love and left him standing there troubled.

But it was difficult to calm Bomplang down. When, on his official rounds every morning, he laid my mail on the kitchen table—as a trusted confidant he had a key to the house—and people came whom he had never seen before—bank officials, lawyers, the tax adviser, museum people, and antiquarians—then he looked at me with desperation as though I were about to be hauled away. But he was naturally too proud to ask in the afternoon what the dark-clad gentlemen had wanted from me. He was more zealous in his work than ever before, put things in order, labeled things, added new card catalogues. Of course, I praised him; his salary was raised considerably, too. Occasionally he was so close to me that I almost called him Stanley. Good old Bomplang; well done, Bomplang; where is the card drawer, Bomplang?

Sometimes I was afraid of not being able to conclude my liquidation, as I called my present activity, before my departure. Particularly the notary public, with whom I was discussing my last will, constantly mentioned new risks that had to be considered in regard to the bequests, so that I had to ask him for the nth time to imagine that I was already dead. "That would simplify the matter," the man said, who with every new document presented a new invoice for fear I could suddenly die without having paid him. You see, the will was to be executed by another lawyer, since I hoped in that way to be safe from crooked business.

Hard work. On the outside, nothing changed; the house still belonged to me, as did the garden, the books—but underneath, in the background, everything was already empty, cleaned out, planned for. And Bomplang, whose entire ambition was to lengthen and beautify my days, worked on the liquidation unwittingly. But what was I supposed to do?

At the beginning of October I went to my bank. It was a clear autumn day, the trees had decided to separate from their leaves. I was in a miserable state, blood pressure too high, too little sleep, and in addition one of my few remaining teeth, which had to support many others, began to hurt. "You've got to stick it out," I had said to myself during the morning over the cup of tea, a cup without a handle that I had thought of not washing again until my departure.

Now I wanted to get the oilcloth notebook, then to decide whether I should take it with me to Corfu or not. If I were to burn it tonight in the fireplace, then, whatever might happen in Corfu, there would no longer be a single documentary proof of my offense. If I left it in the bank, then after twenty years—always assuming there would still be people interested in literary matters and not only people of the type of the new owner of the house—an essay might perhaps appear in the newspaper that would call the authorship of my chief work into question. In spite of my ailments I had to laugh when I imagined the face of that future academician who, after careful investigation, came to the at first cautiously expressed conjecture that a different writer, unfortunately not identifiable, must be the author of the book that in the decade of the fifties of the previous century had had large printings and enjoyed great popularity.

"Down with posthumous fame"—with those words I entered the bank and had myself conducted into the vault, where, at a precise distance from an employee, who had to behold a potential robber even in an eighty-year-old man, I was led to my safe deposit box and took the oilcloth notebook out of it, closed it again, was led upstairs and outside, and set out homeward again, pressing the valuable property to my chest. I neither opened it up nor felt the inclination to read it. It was there, before me, an incunabulum from another age. Now and again I tapped it with my finger, which I then put to my nose, but a specific odor was not to be discovered.

Now that everything was done, time slowed down. There was nothing more to do. In the afternoon Bomplang came, whom I requested to hand the house key over to me. He did so, trembling violently. I poured it all out, in a literal sense, with wine for him, one of the best bottles in the house. Then I showed him the small library that was meant for him, and a small box besides, in which I had gathered a few things for him: two good magnifying glasses, necktie stickpins, cuff links, my grandfather's gold watch, a garnet brooch that had somehow come into my hands, a leather case with dollar bills, and a few other things. It was like Christmas. Tearfully he took every piece into his hands and had me explain where I got it and what it meant to me. When I handed him a diamond pin, he wanted to give it back to me no matter what because it suited me so well—he had noticed that on my eightieth birthday.

"And when may I expect your return, sir?" he asked me when we were packing a few articles of clothing in my light suitcase: two suits, shirts, underclothing—for this trip I did not need a lot.

"You take care of the new owner of the house," I answered him, "especially the wife, who will need your help."

Alone again, I spent the last night in my house. I used everything with great care, as though nothing more belonged to me. I turned off the faucet particularly tightly.

Because I could not sleep I took another walk "around to all four corners." I walked to the bench where I had sat for the last time with Stanley, sat down a moment, but was too restless to give way to my thoughts while sitting. I walked to the art museum, which was dark and threatening, then made a curve around the Feldherrnhalle and then, suddenly breathing heavily, abruptly walked back up LudwigstraBe. Around two o'clock in the morning I was back home again, bathed in sweat. I lay down under a light blanket on my sofa in the library with my clothes on and waited for sleep.

XVII

T HERE IS a single photograph of Leo and me, a
yellowed, creased document with dog-eared corners that
I have saved over the years. Why are there no further
proofs of our journey? I had looked through the nega-
tives again and again as to whether or not chance had
united both of us in a picture, but found no example.
Only this photograph, which has an unusual story.

An Englishman, who was researching the death rituals of the Indians, had with his wife stopped at our camp
and invited us to accompany them to a tribe three days'
journey away that had, as they knew from earlier visits,

a set of musical instruments that were used exclusively at funeral ceremonies. Against my initial resistance, which I had attempted to justify with overwork, we finally rode with them and, to the great joy of the English couple, reached the village at the very moment when it was preparing for the burial of a person of rank.

When he felt his strength failing, the man had lain down on a bed and informed the village of his coming demise. So, when we entered, a dozen Indians were squatting as though faraway all around the dying man, who for his part only occasionally emitted a rattle from his throat that was noted by the group with sudden squealing wails. On the other hand, when the man was finally dead, there began such a furious noise that I wished I were right back in my camp, where death rituals ordinarily took place under the Christian eye of the priest in a somewhat civilized way.

But here it was the three sons of the old man who behaved like madmen, pulled out their hair and scratched the skin all over their bodies, struck out wildly all about and with bare feet stomped the fire, all the while roaring as though not in their right senses and letting their tears flow until, like good actors, they suddenly collapsed and lay like jerking bundles. But the rest of the

dwellers in the village had just been waiting for this moment, because for their part they were now allowed to set
loose such a cacophony of moans and screams that it
turned the stomach of any amiable observer. Then along
with this ritual the promised instruments also came into
play finally, even though the tones they produced had
very little to do with music. They were noise instruments.

I stood there helplessly as half-naked women threw
themselves bawling onto the corpse and ripped it and bit
it until it looked squalid and bedraggled, which then
called a third group of people into action, who with cries
tied up the bundle with all kinds of bast, and gave it to
some extent a proper shape again. Meanwhile, at the
edge of the village square, a grave had been dug to which
the corpse was to be carried—and at that moment the
Englishman's wife, untroubled by the noise and insensi-
tive to the mourning of the entire population of the village, pressed the shutter.

I got up again and took the photograph out from
under mountains of old papers, knowing well where it
was located. It shows the self-assured musicological ethnologist with crossed arms, a tropical helmet on his head,
tight riding pants, and an expression on his face as
though he were listening to a concert by the Philhar-

monic, and next to him me with arms pressed in fright close to my body, wide-open eyes and gaping mouth, and finally, Leo. He is kneeling to my right, his hat pushed onto his brow, and has a frightened young ape in his arms, which he was trying to shelter from the noise. He, too, is looking up into the camera, as though he had been requested to do so.

And now, when I inspect the photograph and even seek the aid of my magnifying glass in order to grasp it in all its details, as though it contained the secret of our existence, as though it were a rare proof of our precarious duality, I also again hear the cry of the Englishwoman, who was not content to photograph only Leo's body but also wanted to have his face. So he had looked up with a serious expression. And now I remember that there had been something between the Englishwoman and Leo, just a brief episode because of the shortness of the trip and the presence of the husband, about which no words had been wasted, but which had happened. And I see him now—somewhat through the photograph—at the attendant celebration, which ended in a drinking bout, sitting next to the Englishwoman, laughing and singing, while I had to take a seat next to a stinking old man who, babbling toothlessly, was trying to tell me a fairy tale

Himmelfarb

about a higher being, of which I, however, understood hardly anything. The Englishman had been done in by the corn beer. He was sleeping off his intoxication next to a few Indians in a hut, which I likewise sought out later I, too, badly drunk. The next morning the Englishwoman and Leo were also present. They lay side by side next to the entrance, covered by Leo's broad cloak, and were holding hands in their sleep. When many years later my book had appeared in English translation, the musicologist's wife sent me the photograph, with the request that I make a copy of it for my friend and traveling companion, whose name she had unfortunately forgotten.

In order to bring to a halt the memories that now assailed me, I tore the photograph in half and then again, but then did not throw it into the wastebasket after all but stuck the scraps into an envelope on which I wrote "Leo Himmelfarb." Let future generations guess who the three young men were and what event brought them together in this photograph.

184

XVIII

WHEN HAD I last flown?

I was sitting in first class, being served by a young woman who constantly brought me new surprises. Hot washcloths, cognac, fruit juices, newspapers—if I had asked her to tell me the story of her life, she would also have done that for me because I was the only patient in her closed-off compartment. But I didn't want to hear anything. A wonderful vacuum filled me, if that paradox is permitted.

It was the fourteenth of October, and in Athens, where I had to change planes, it was still quite warm. The city was cooling down only slowly after a hot summer. By taxi I had myself driven at a breakneck speed to the National Airport, and because there were supposedly construction sites all over the place, the man, to whom I had incautiously given my departure time, drove all over the city. "Acropolis," said the driver, and dutifully and bored I cast a brief glance up at the high field of ruins that was crumbling away in a cloud of smog. In all my visits here I have never been able to imagine that in this very city—which seemed to consist of generally dangerous taxi drivers, honking, cursing steering-wheel fanatics in dilapidated cars—democracy had once been invented, but what I saw now of cheap tinsel, advertisements, and dirt caused me to close my eyes. I have the right not to have to look at everything, I told myself, which seemed to give the crazy guy behind the wheel the right to pull the wool completely over my eyes, me, the dozing old man from Germany. I paid him. I also paid the porter who carried my suitcase, even tipped the adolescent who tossed my light, far-traveled satchel like a piece of carrion onto the conveyor belt. Just take everything, there's plenty there. Remember me well.

In the small propeller-driven airplane that took me to Corfu there was no first class, for which reason I, the old man, had to sit in the middle between two boors who were companions and taken together were about half as old as I but for incomprehensible reasons could not sit in the middle. "I can sit only at the window," the one told me voluntarily and pulled down the shade, "my friend only on the aisle," which did not prevent them, by the way, from talking past my head constantly, in English— presumably foreign Greeks. Sitting, as it were, at the junction of a fervent exchange about love affairs, I permitted myself a few of my own paltry thoughts concerning the senselessness and stupidity of arguments, but came to no conclusions. "Nothing can be learned"; with that sigh I withdrew into myself and soon became lost as well in the gloomy caverns of sleep.

But this uncomfortable trip, too, came to an end, and I enjoyed being picked up by a civilized driver from the hotel. Tinted glass, air conditioner, a string quartet by whomever, in any event Central European. The island was still green. Cascades of blossoms hung over the walls. A light breeze was blowing that swirled the leaves of the olive trees silvery. I was seated happily on the backseat, my briefcase with the oilcloth notebook on my lap, looking, looking, looking.

The hotel is even more pleasant than I remembered.

Himmelfarb

Years ago I had been invited to give a lecture here before a learned society about the relationship of Kaiser Wilhelm II to the colonies. Just exactly why I was worthy enough to be chosen to speak about Wilhelm, with whom the other participants of the conference were more or less on intimate terms in a good as well as a bad sense, remained a mystery to me, but I acquitted myself of my task, received a sumptuous honorarium, and at the expense of some rich American, who had been overwhelmed by Wilhelm's uniform, spent a splendid week in this hotel.

Now I even remember the rest of the speakers, too. One of them was a Dr. Zombusch from Berlin, a nasty moocher of the intelligent sort who carried on exclusively and unendingly in a broad, nasal tone about Wilhelm's supposed homosexuality and quite by chance never had a drachma with him when we had to pay for our drinks. The other was a thoroughly cynical, constantly drunk English historian, the enfant terrible of the Oxford Historical Society, as they said to me behind his back to justify the man's actually frightful consumption of whiskey. In contrast to the conceited Zombusch, he was a brilliant conversationalist and, hanging around me, could dress down the other participants of the conference either openly or covertly so unmercifully that I, a stranger in this academic milieu, took great delight in it. When he was intoxicated, he forgot what language we were speaking, ordered more wine in Polish, cursed in Russian, and then sang a German drinking song. Chamisso spoke in Hawaiian in a coma, but this intelligent drinker had no understanding for Chamisso's coma. I later sent him the English edition of one of my books and received from him a relentless but cordial letter that culminated with the suggestion that the translation probably had been done by one of the Indians I had described so realistically as being incapable of a clear thought.

Pale, eternally pale Englishmen were sitting in the air-conditioned lobby, reading *The Times*. A dark brown hued German married couple wearing blue shorts handed each another *Die Welt* back and forth. Waiters in white jackets brought drinks. After my luggage was stored in my room, I chose an easy chair in a corner from which I had my eye on the entrance through which Leo would come tomorrow. After fifty years, I wanted to see him first.

At the reception desk I had had them give me the

flights from Israel to Athens, with the connecting flights, and was sure that he would have to arrive about two o'clock in the afternoon, in the heat of midday, if he did not come with the evening plane, and would take the last inland flight so that I would be able to greet him only after supper. But that seemed unlikely to me.

I ordered a milky ouzo with ice and a sandwich, and read a few pages from the memoirs of Somerset Maugham which I had bought in the airport.

It just now occurs to me that it's the only book that I still own. It is a nice feeling not to have anything anymore, no books, no furniture, no house, no family. Just some money in my wallet, a paperback by Somerset Maugham, a few memories, a briefcase with an old oil-cloth notebook, and this journal. And a second ouzo, which tasted better to me than the first and coated the inside of my mouth.

Slightly giddy I went to my room and at the open window listened to the cicadas, to their chaotic, frenetic songs. The air in the room was stuffy. So, to get over an attack of weakness, I had to close my eyes. And suddenly I was in the primal forest again, suddenly I was fighting my way with Leo through the underbrush, yelling loudly to frighten away the animals. We had been delayed after an excursion, the day was ending already, and we were more than four kilometers away from our camp, if we could believe the surveys. Except that in the falling darkness we were no longer sure in what direction we should go. Leo suggested that we separate. He wanted to try farther to the south; I was to keep going in my direction, and whoever arrived at camp first should look for the other with reinforcements. I fought my way on doggedly, all around me the dull buzzing and humming of insects in the darkness, the bellowing of apes, and the bleating sounds of other invisible animals. Sometime or other I must have fallen down and remained lying there. I see myself lying there and waving away attackers with hands growing tired, hearing the rustling behind my back, the enraged cries of the inhabitants of this darkness who were trying to drive off the nocturnal disturber of their peace. And finally the laughing face of Leo, who had naturally taken the right path, and our friends, who had finally found me and carried me, dirtied and bitten, into camp on a litter.

I must have nodded off while sitting, for a hotel employee was standing suddenly next to me, asking whether I was ill. It was still hot in the room; my body was soaked with sweat. The young man opened the bed and had to wait a long time before I understood that he expected a tip, and when I had finally given him a much-too-large bill, he felt obliged to arrange this and that before he could again disappear.

Probably I have busied myself too long with death to expect anything of it. It will always be unjust, and it will be final, without a mask. The Indians believed, contrary to the awful priest with his heavenly promises, that the dead would always be nearby, in the bush, beneath the roots of a tree, in the water of the river. You had to watch out that you didn't step on them, else they would kick back. Leo had written down many conversations with them about death, which you can read in my books. Something always occurred to these people about death, and even Leo was in fine fettle when he could talk about it. "Not the fear of death makes us think about immortality, rather the wish for immortality provokes the fear of death," he often quoted from an Austrian philosopher. "The awareness of death, of mortality, is the beginning of all storytelling" was one of his comments when I no longer knew what to say.

Now I no longer knew what to say.

I was sitting on the edge of the bed in my undershirt, my feet set pedantically next to one another. As though stuck in concrete. Had someone demanded that I stand up, I couldn't have done it. In front of me a chasm, so deep that I could not see its bottom from the bed's edge. And no bridge, no gangway, not even a loose plank over which I could have left the realm of solitude. With horror I discovered that I had also lost words; only a croak came when I opened my mouth, a croak of shame and remorse. Only my brain seemed still to function, even though in accordance with a scheme I did not know. It perceived something, assimilated it, but the result was such that I could draw no salutary conclusions. Over my whole body I felt an invisible, sticky net, which slowly drew tighter.

When it began to get light, the tension relaxed. I could see again. Slowly, with small sips, I drank a glass of water. The trembling with which the night had smitten my body—a slight, constant trembling, interrupted at intervals by the most violent despondency and boundless agitation—gave way to an exhaustion that slackened my limbs. Finally I was able to let myself sink onto the bed and stretch out my legs. So I lay there unmoving. Life could not do much of anything with me; death had nothing planned for me. Only a miserable dissatisfaction was sitting on my chest like a beast. Apologies also were of no help. Suddenly I had to laugh. I had never earned anything in my life, had always simply taken. And what I had taken turned into dust under my laughter.

XIX

LEO HAD A FEVER. His brow burned and produced more and more beads of sweat that ran down the sides like bubbles and soaked his hair that hung disordered and tangled over his ears. He looked like a fountain, but sometime or other he would be empty, dried up. We had wrapped his emaciated body in a broad-woven cloth, laid him on a rough wooden bed with high ends that was standing in the middle of the room because the holes in the walls were full of vermin and he didn't like to lie in the hammock—It prevented him from breathing deeply. At the door I had posted an Indian woman who was supposed to prevent the entrance of people and animals. At a terrible drinking bout followed by a fight she had lost an eye—not only an eye but also a part of her senses. She babbled constantly to herself, a glib visionary from whose dark lips words sprang unchecked. "She has wild ideas," said Leo, who had healed her festering eyes.

She had leaned her back stiffly against the wall, a framework made up of tightly woven twigs and smeared with clay that crumbled in the sun and ran off when it rained. She spoke with insulting disparagement about anyone who came close to the house, especially about the priest, to deride whom she brought forth rich offerings of words because he attributed laziness, dissoluteness, and untruthfulness to her. She was also the caretaker of a smoldering fire that was supposed to drive away flies that, however, seemed to be resistant to it. At any rate, I had my hands full shooing away the pestiferous insects who wanted to take their nourishment from my sweat-soaked companion.

I had placed my chair so that I could see past Leo and the one-eyed old woman to the entrance whose bright square had the effect of a movie screen. I knew the film, in spite of the many tiny changes that were made daily in the script. Sometimes the actors entered from the left, with bundles of twigs or bunches of bananas on their shoulders; sometimes they came from the depths of the center of the picture and turned off shortly before the house, as though they had an inner aversion to push through the screen. Sometimes they stopped in the middle of the square and began one of their unendingly long conversations that suddenly, as though from an acute lack of words, was broken off.

When I bring that image to mind, how I sat day after day in that dark tropical movie house, Leo before me as though mummified in his woven cloth, groaning at ever shorter intervals, the old witch at the door in the acrid smoke of herbs, and on the village square the curiously inaccessible life of our colony, then my recollection opens all the doors and lets into the house of my memories all the images, sounds, smells, colors, and words of which my existence consisted at the time. And now I see before me how I bend over Leo's dwindling, no longer resisting body because he suddenly begins to speak, crazy, disconnected words, until he is again reclaimed by quiet.

"Christ never laughed" was one of the sentences that now occurred to me. "You have to suck at the ears of a Christian until they begin to swell. Priests are of the opinion that celibacy means polygamy, and the Indians are so devout that they can serve several religions without difficulty." With a monotone voice he attacked the truth of the revelation and denied the existence of God.

So it kept on. A gloomy torrent made its way through the dark lodging, so that even the old slattern stopped her singsong and came shuffling over to convince herself of the change in the condition of our sick man.

"*Licenca para um homem de paz*," she whispered to me and began to giggle. A gurgling giggle rose in her that changed into a loud bleating, then she threw herself onto the ground and rubbed dirt in her face. "What do I approach?" she cried out with sobs. "I approach battered flesh, burst arteries, splintered bones." And finally she began to draw a circle around the sickbed with her outstretched finger, drew a man inside it, and bored him through several times fiercely with her foot.

That night the fever decreased. The next morning Leo asked me to fetch the oilcloth notebook, and in addition a new account book and writing utensils, since he wanted to start to dictate the description of our journey to me. He was still feeble and infirm, and his yellow-flecked eyes still glowed feverishly, but his energy, which had kept me alive at the time, flickered up again so that mornings and evenings we could work for several hours one after the other. I wrote like a madman in order to catch every word, and after a month his and my report was done.

XX

LEO DIDN'T COME. Not with the early, nor with the late airplane. This morning I took a long walk along the ocean with the oilcloth notebook under my arm. In a small restaurant—four tables on a covered summer terrace—I ate a squid, which the innkeeper had just caught and before my eyes had beat at least a hundred times with a rock, and drank a glass of cold wine with it. I was alone. Before me the geometry of the waves that continually re-formed in spite of the wind. An east wind.

For a brief moment I felt, as always on the ocean, the tug of a longing that comes from the region of the heart and squeezes my body as though under very high tension. At once my memories conspired against me. I got up quickly and paid in order to recover my composure while walking. Heavy heartbeats that reminded me of a so-called heart hysteria that had bothered me once in Rome. Fear? I broke off a stalk of rosemary and picked a few mint leaves that I rubbed between my fingers. Before, when I still had a house, I brought herbs, stones, mussels, and that sort of thing home with me from my journeys. The whole house was full of these holy things. Now I had to lay aside a new supply.

I found a place protected from the wind which I liberated from the remains of the summer: plastic bottles, countless shoes and sandals—as though at this very spot a great crowd of people had taken farewell forever from the continent—suntan lotion containers, and other colorful objects that obviously no one missed.

I proceeded with a care that surprised even me. I covered the heap of trash with a page of the *Corriere* that had turned brown and which an Italian had buried only after a fashion, and weighed it down with rocks. Behind me stood a group of sweet-smelling beach lilies that looked like they had just been stuck into the sand dune. "Like a fresh grave" went through my head. Above me a loving pair of doves; still higher a jet fighter that gave the blue sky a zipper.

I watch a couple of ants that with maddening busyness go about their work, even here on the beach, and while I watch them I feel myself observed. Someone is nearby, a living creature follows all my actions. I felt it so clearly that I would not have been surprised to see somebody, but no one showed himself. Unpleasant, and finally even threatening.

So I stand up again, leave the sheltered place, and move to a small stand of stone pines, the only possible hiding place. There stood the observer, tied fast to a tree, its ears perked up, its eyes wide open, as is proper for a detective. A donkey, a wonderful gray donkey that now, in greeting, emits an aspirated sound, half shout of joy, half scream of torment, in any case a signal that was meant only for me and understood only by me.

Back in my niche I took out my notebook, in which I have captured this report, in order to bring it to a conclusion. Remarkable, I've reached the next to last page.

How often I had allowed myself postponements because I had kept hoping to bring a bit of clarity into my affairs. But there is no clarity, only the theft, the stolen hour. I'm not even strong enough to commence a capitulation. I don't want to write anymore. This notebook, too, shall have a blank page, a page for itself. Right away, I will put it, together with a photograph of Stanley and me in the English Garden, in my briefcase and then I will set that weighed down with a stone on one of the boulders that lie like tired animals on the sand. The briefcase shall be visible to those who wish to see it.

May someone find it who is interested in humankind.

The sun is rising; soon the vacationers will come. I have to hurry. I am sitting so motionless that the lizards creep up to my shoes, with high-rearing, listening little heads. It is now 11:45. Now there is still room for one word: